'Do you hav
on me?' Abl

'I'm good at my
overseer.'

'I never thought for one minute you did,' he said. 'I just want to see everything, and I thought you'd be the logical person to shadow. Dr Lawrie must have come on your rounds with you, surely?'

'Yes, but he was—' She pulled herself up short.

'A friend?' he finished for her. 'Can't we be friends, Abby?'

Maggie Kingsley lives with her family in a remote cottage in the north of Scotland surrounded by sheep and deer. She is from a family with a strong medical tradition, and has enjoyed a varied career including lecturing and working for a major charity, but writing has always been her first love. When not writing she combines working for an employment agency with her other interest, interior design.

Recent titles by the same author:

A QUESTION OF TRUST

A TIME
TO CHANGE

BY
MAGGIE KINGSLEY

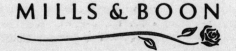

MILLS & BOON

*MILLS & BOON, the Rose Device and
LOVE ON CALL are trademarks of the publisher.
Harlequin Mills & Boon Limited,
Eton House, 18-24 Paradise Road, Richmond, Surrey TW9 1SR*

© Maggie Kingsley 1996

ISBN 0 263 79628 0

*Set in Times 10 on 11 pt. by
Rowland Phototypesetting Limited
Bury St Edmunds, Suffolk*

03-9607-49473

Made and printed in Great Britain

CHAPTER ONE

'WHAT do you suppose he'll look like, Abby?' Carol declared thoughtfully.

'Like a man, I guess,' Abby replied, helping herself to a glass of white wine and some sandwiches from the buffet, though even just the thought of eating anything tonight was enough to make her feel quite sick. 'Two arms, two legs, a body, a head. . .'

'That's not what I meant and you know it!' Carol Lennox laughed as they made their way through the crush of invited guests gathered on the lawn outside Ardmar Children's Hospital. 'You must be just a little bit curious about him, surely? I mean it's not every day we get a new boss, a new boss whose job—'

She came to a sudden halt, her cheeks crimson with clear embarrassment.

'A new boss whose job I thought I'd get?' Abby finished for her with an unsteady laugh. 'Don't look so stricken, Carol. It's true—I did think I'd get the job. With Alastair Bell being just newly qualified and Joe Ferguson not wanting promotion, I thought I was the natural choice.'

'You're only thirty, Abby. Molly told me this Dr Maguire's thirty-six.'

'No one thought Tim Collins too young to be appointed chief of staff at Norwood and he's the same age as me.'

'Yes, but. . .'

'He's a man?' Abby suggested with a tinge of bitterness. 'Indeed he is. And now you must excuse me, Carol—I really should circulate.'

5

She turned quickly on her heel, though the last thing she wanted to do this evening was circulate, and walked straight into the very person she had been trying to avoid all night—George Benson, owner of Benson's Farm Fresh Chickens, and the most vocal member of Ardmar's board of governors.

'Well, this is a grand night, isn't it, Dr Hunter?' he declared, his portly frame barring her escape. 'For our little hospital to have attracted a man of Sean Maguire's calibre—holder of a first-class honours degree from Dublin University, experienced in working in two of London's finest hospitals, author of three books on paediatric care. . .'

'Walks on water and performs the odd miracle in his spare time?' Abby muttered, taking a deep gulp of her wine and wishing it were halfway drinkable so that she could spend the rest of the evening getting quietly and completely drunk.

'What did you say, Dr Hunter?' George queried with a slight frown.

'I said it makes you wonder why a man like Dr Maguire should even consider coming here at all, doesn't it?' she said sweetly.

He nodded vigorously, clearly oblivious to her sarcasm. 'I just hope you're not too disappointed yourself, my dear,' he continued. 'You did a grand job, keeping the hospital ticking along nicely after Dr Lawrie's sad death, but when it came to replacing him on a permanent basis I felt—that is, the board and I felt,' he added hurriedly, 'that we needed someone quite exceptional.'

He was right the first time, she thought acidly. She knew damn well that without William Lawrie to champion her cause the rest of the board had followed George's lead like the load of sheep they were, and when he'd said he wanted someone quite exceptional he'd meant a man.

'You're a good little worker—none better,' George beamed. 'And if you keep up the good work—well, who knows what giddy heights you might aspire to?'

Abby muttered something incomprehensible in reply and fled. Dear God, she thought furiously as she took refuge in a quiet corner of the lawn, she was a highly qualified and experienced doctor, for heaven's sake, and yet if she had stayed for much longer George Benson would probably have patted her on the head.

It was so unfair, so damned unfair, she thought, glaring at the large banner inscribed 'Welcome Dr Maguire' hanging over the hospital's front door. The chief of staff's job was hers by right—she knew it was. Why else had William Lawrie given her such a free hand if it was not because he was grooming her to replace him? Why else had he consulted her so often if it was not because he saw her as the future head of the hospital?

'I miss him too, my dear.'

Abby turned to see William's widow gazing sympathetically at her and swallowed hard. 'Ardmar isn't going to be the same without him, Jean.'

A shadow passed across Jean Lawrie's lined face for an instant and then she smiled. 'You'll like Sean Maguire, Abby—I know I did when I met him in London.'

Abby bit into one of her sandwiches without enthusiasm and wondered if there was anyone she would meet tonight who would not sing this man's praises.

'I must say, you're looking very nice tonight, my dear,' Jean continued, deliberately changing the conversation.

'Nice'. Not pretty, not lovely, but 'nice'. What a world of tact there was in that one word. 'Nice' meant you'd done the best you could with what attributes you had and Abby had never had any illusions about her attributes.

Her chin was too square, her cheekbones were too wide, and her hair wasn't the Titian or auburn beloved of painters but red—bright, fiery red and stubbornly curly. She'd struggled for an hour and a half this evening to subdue it into a stylishly sleek bob, but the warmth in the June sun had already teased it back into its customary mass of wayward curls.

Surreptitiously she glanced across at her reflection in the large ground-floor windows opposite and sighed. It had been a mistake to wear her green silk dress. She looked, she decided wryly, like an upside-down carrot.

'Have you seen Robert this evening?' Jean continued, scanning the crowd with interest.

Abby shook her head. 'Knowing Robert, he's probably got so involved with some physiotherapy problem that he's forgotten what day of the week it is, let alone that we're all supposed to be here to welcome Dr Maguire.'

Jean chuckled. 'Poor Robert—he is a bit forgetful at times but I like him.'

'Everyone does.'

Jean glanced at her sideways. 'When are you going to marry him, Abby?'

'Arranging a wedding takes time. . .'

'Two years?' Jean protested. 'That's how long you've been engaged, you know. I'm beginning to wonder if you really want to marry him at all.'

Abby stared down into her glass of wine. 'I'm very fond of him. . .'

'I'm fond of lots of people but that doesn't mean I'd want to marry them,' Jean observed. 'Marrying Robert would give you security, comfort, and for some women that would be enough, but I think you need more. I think you need a man who can make you laugh.'

Abby gazed at her in stunned silence for a moment and then broke into a peal of laughter. 'I've heard of lots of reasons for marrying someone, but never that!'

'I'm being serious,' Jean declared. 'You're an intelligent girl, a gifted doctor. You don't need to marry someone for security, but you do need some laughter in your life. Robert—'

'I think Finlay Norris is trying to attract your attention,' Abby said quickly, waving to the tall, grey-haired man opposite.

'Abby—'

'I wouldn't keep him waiting. William always said Finlay was one of that very rare breed—a businessman with a conscience. Who knows? He might be thinking of increasing his donation to the hospital this year.'

Jean's lips curved into a wry smile. 'You're getting better and better at avoiding subjects you don't want to discuss, my dear, but don't think this means I've given up on you, because I haven't!'

Jean meant well, Abby thought as she watched her walk across the lawn, but surely being fond of someone was a good enough reason to marry them? Sometimes she thought it was. Sometimes in the loneliness of the night she had almost convinced herself it was. Robert loved her and he would never hurt her. At times he might drive her to distraction with his easygoing manner, but he would never hurt her. And loving someone didn't always bring happiness. It could bring heartache and pain—she of all people should know that.

'This evening's turning into a complete non-event as far as I'm concerned,' Carol grumbled as she joined her. 'No sign of the guest of honour, and do you know what George Benson had the nerve to ask me? He said he hoped I'd made sure Dr Maguire's cottage was in tip-top shape for him. I'm a staff nurse for heaven's sake, not a cleaner!'

'George doesn't always recognise the difference,' Abby sighed, dragging her mind back to the present with difficulty.

'What could have happened to Dr Maguire, do you suppose?' Carol continued. 'Could he have got lost?'

'It would appear not,' Abby said drily as a gleaming black Porsche suddenly tore up the driveway and then slewed to a halt in front of the main building in a shower of gravel. 'It would appear that Dr Maguire simply likes to make an entrance.'

'Well, that was some entrance,' Carol breathed, her hand going up to her blonde curls automatically as the car door was thrown open and a man got out. 'And that, I have to say, is one very good-looking man.'

He was. Sean Maguire was tall and muscular with a shock of thick black hair. Laughter-lines were etched round his deep grey eyes but there was no sign of laughter on his dark face at the moment and for a split second Abby wondered if he could possibly be nervous and then dismissed the thought. No man who looked as good as Sean Maguire did could ever be nervous.

'Would you just look at the cut of his suit?' Carol continued, her blue eyes sparkling in admiration. 'It's got to be Italian, don't you think? And that tie—that tie's silk, isn't it?'

And his shoes are probably Gucci, Abby thought with derision. Sean Maguire couldn't have been small, fat and bald, could he? It wasn't enough that he had qualifications a mile long, he had to look as though he'd stepped out of a fashion magazine as well. No wonder he had impressed the board at his interview. If they'd issued an Identikit profile of the ideal man for the job they couldn't have done better.

'Let's introduce ourselves,' Carol urged.

'In a minute,' Abby replied, but Carol hadn't even heard her; she had already gone.

Anyone would think he was Moses bringing the tablets of stone down from the mountainside, Abby thought with a surge of irritation as she watched the assembled crowd rush towards Dr Maguire. Only she was standing back; only she was gazing at him critically. And that's because only you are suffering from a very bad case of sour grapes, her mind told her firmly.

Well, so what if she was? So what if common sense told her that it wasn't Sean Maguire's fault that he'd been appointed chief of staff, nor his fault that he was good-looking, nor his fault that he was a man. He was going to have to prove himself to be one heck of an administrator before she was going to forgive him for his success, and if that was childish and petty, then childish and petty she intended to be.

'What are you doing hiding back here?' Jean asked, appearing without warning at her side. 'Come and meet Sean.'

'No—really—I'd rather wait a while,' Abby protested, but it was no use. Jean had her in a remarkably tight grip for someone so small, and other than wrenching her arm free there was nothing Abby could do but go with her.

'Sean, I'd like to introduce you to my very favourite member of staff,' Jean smiled, pushing her forward deliberately.

He'd been deep in conversation with Carol, who was blushing prettily at something he'd said, but he turned towards Abby immediately, clear interest on his face.

'If this is your favourite member of staff, Jean, it's got to be Abby Hunter,' he said with a smile. 'I'm delighted to meet you, Abby.'

His soft Irish accent was charming, the candour in

his grey eyes appealing, and yet Abby stiffened. Somewhere in the back of her mind a warning bell sounded, somewhere in the darkest recesses of her brain a memory stirred, but she couldn't for the life of her think what had prompted it.

'According to Jean there's nothing you don't know about Ardmar,' he continued, 'so I'm afraid I'm going to be beating a path to your door until I find my feet around here.'

She pulled herself together sharply. Why the hell should she help him? He'd got the job; it was up to him if he sank or swam.

'You can certainly beat a path to my door,' she replied evenly, 'but whether I'll be there is another matter—I do have my own duties to attend to, you know.'

'Of course,' he said, his black eyebrows narrowing slightly, 'but you'll be able to spare me just a little of your time, surely?'

'I have a very full schedule. . .' she began, and then, conscious that Jean was frowning at her, added hurriedly, 'But I'll do what I can.'

'How very generous of you,' he replied drily, and Abby flushed.

She was behaving badly—she knew she was—but there was something about him—something oddly familiar though she knew they'd never met—that was making her decidedly uncomfortable.

'You must be hungry after your long drive from London, Dr Maguire,' Carol declared, glancing from him to Abby in clear bewilderment. 'Would you like me to get you something from the buffet?'

He shook his head. 'I had a meal at a motorway service station on my way up.'

'Probably very wise,' Jean observed.

Sean's eyebrows rose. 'The food's not good?'

'George Benson has organised Ardmar's functions for as long as anyone can remember,' Jean sighed, 'and his menus are—how shall I phrase this tactfully? Somewhat limited?'

He grinned. 'Then it's clearly time Mr Benson was relieved of his onerous responsibility. I'll put that at the top of my agenda.'

Something inside Abby snapped. 'Considering you're scarcely in the door, I wouldn't have thought you'd have had time to find anything you want to change—far less been able to make out an agenda!'

He gazed at her steadily. 'New brooms always find a few things they'd like to change, don't they?'

'Yes, but normally they wait a decent interval,' she retorted.

'This isn't the time or the place for such a conversation, Abby,' Jean murmured warningly, aware that several of the guests were staring at them.

'It's all right, Jean,' Sean said smoothly. 'I can assure Abby that I don't intend to do anything radical. My main priority is to keep Ardmar open. The money Sir Duncan Munroe invested in the 1920s to create a children's hospital is fast running out. The NHS won't help us—they'd like nothing better than to shut us down and ship all our patients to Inverness.'

He was right, but that did not make it any easier for Abby to swallow.

'And how do you propose to safeguard us—by closing the day centre, making staff cuts?' she asked.

'By increasing public donations.'

Abby shook her head. 'Most of the local businesses and wealthier members of the community already give very generously—'

'And several give nothing at all, according to the annual reports,' he broke in. 'I'm also considering hosting a few special events in the grounds to raise more capital.'

'Pop concerts and the like?' she said sarcastically.

'Why not? We need money—'

'Not that badly, surely?' she interrupted, horrified.

'That badly, yes,' he said, his voice hardening. 'And if I discover that the only way to keep this hospital afloat is to have striptease dancers in every weekend, then striptease dancers we will have and you'll just have to get used to the idea.'

The threat in his words was clear. Ardmar was his now, to do with as he chose, and he would brook no interference. How in the world was she ever going to work for this man? she wondered unhappily. She might just as well give him her resignation right now.

'Are you sure I can't get you anything from the buffet, Sean?' Jean said brightly, glancing from Abby's red cheeks to his set face uncomfortably. 'I know I was critical of the food. . .'

'I'm more tired than hungry,' he replied. 'There was an accident on the motorway and I stopped to do what I could—that's why I was so late.'

'Then what on earth are you doing here?' she exclaimed. 'Get yourself off to your cottage. Abby will show you the way—won't you, Abby?'

Sean thought that the only place Abby Hunter looked willing to take him at the moment was the top of the nearest cliff and shook his head. 'I'd better stay, Jean. Mr Benson and the board have gone to a lot of trouble organising this welcome party—'

'Nonsense!' she interrupted. 'I'll deal with George Benson—you two run along.'

Sean knew perfectly well what Jean was up to. She was clearly hoping that if he and Abby spent some time together they might find some common ground— and they had to find some common ground and quickly. Ardmar was too small a place for personality clashes.

'Well, if you think it will be OK, and Abby wouldn't mind. . .?' he said, letting his question hang in the air.

'Of course she doesn't mind,' Jean smiled before Abby could say anything. 'Perhaps you'd like to walk—stretch your legs? It's not far and our handyman could take your car down for you.'

Sean gazed at Abby thoughtfully. He had expected a certain coolness from her, given that they'd both applied for the same post, but Abby Hunter wasn't simply cool—she was positively arctic. Surely somewhere underneath that icy exterior there was a likeable human being, or else why had Jean sung her praises so highly? He made up his mind.

'Stretching my legs sounds a great idea.'

Abby groaned inwardly. To be stuck in the car with him for ten minutes would have been bad enough, but to have to endure his company for a full half-hour was the absolute limit. She glanced across at him with barely disguised annoyance and for a split second almost thought she saw amusement in his grey eyes. So he found this situation funny, did he? Well, let him just see how amusing he found it after she'd taken him the quick way to his cottage—that would wipe the smile off his face and the polish off his fancy shoes!

'Aren't we going by the road?' he asked as she set off across the lawn without a word, leaving him to follow her.

'This is a short-cut.'

'Anxious to get rid of me?' he suggested.

'Of course not,' she replied evenly. 'But you said you were tired, so I assumed you'd want to reach your cottage as quickly as possible.'

'How very thoughtful of you.'

The laughter in his voice was unmistakable and

deliberately she quickened her pace, only to find that
he soon lagged far behind her.

'Having trouble?' she asked sweetly when he eventually caught up.

'Don't you ever take the time just to admire the
view?' he protested. 'It's beautiful here.'

She gazed out over the parkland, at the solid towers
of the hospital's main building in the distance, and
nodded. 'I've been here six years and never had any
regrets.'

'Now why should I have the impression that you'd
like to add "until now" to that statement?'

His gaze was direct and she found herself flushing.
Damn and blast the man—he was too sharp by half.
'We'd better press on,' she said. 'You must be wanting
to get settled in.'

'What I want—is to get to know you a little better,'
he said, leaning back against a tree.

'There isn't much to know,' she said stonily.

'Well, I see you're engaged—you could start by telling me who he is and how you came to work here.'

She didn't want to tell him anything about her private life, but with his eyes fixed on her so intently she
knew she had to say something.

'I'm engaged to Robert Forrest—he's head of
our Physiotherapy department. I did my training in
Edinburgh and when a post became vacant at Ardmar I
applied, was accepted, and have been here ever since.'

He longed to ask more, to ask why her eyes
had darkened perceptibly when she'd mentioned
Edinburgh, but instead he smiled and said, 'That
wasn't so very hard, was it?' only to see her face set
into rigid lines.

She wasn't a pretty woman, he decided, but her
direct brown eyes were fringed by incredibly long black
eyelashes and she had the most amazing wealth of red

hair he'd ever seen. If she would only smile he was
sure she could be quite attractive but there was no
laughter in her face just now—none at all. He sighed.
It had been a mistake forcing her into his company.
He was getting nowhere.

'Which way do we go now?' he asked in defeat.

'Along there,' she answered, pointing to the muddy
track ahead.

He frowned. 'Are you sure?'

'We could always go back and ask someone to drive
you if you're tired,' she told him, her expression
innocent.

'I'm not tired, it's just. . .'

'Just what?'

'Nothing—I guess you know what you're doing,' he
declared.

Too true, she thought as she set off down the path.
She had known perfectly well just how muddy this way
was going to be after last week's rain and the prospect
of the immaculate Sean Maguire arriving mud-stained
and exhausted at his cottage had been too good to
pass up. That, at least, had been her plan, but it did
not take her long to discover that if anyone was going
to arrive in that condition it was going to be her. The
way she'd chosen would have been difficult enough in
flat shoes, but it was virtually impossible in high heels.

'Having trouble?' he asked solicitously as she paused
yet again to pull her heels free from the cloying mud.

'No,' she muttered grimly, desperately endeavouring
to keep her balance.

'Good,' he replied, and to her amazement strode
on ahead.

'Where are you going?' she called after him, torn
between dismay and anger.

He stopped. 'This is the right way, isn't it?'

'Yes, but. . .'

'But what?' he asked, coming back to her, a maddening smile playing around his lips. 'Is there a problem?'

Anger flooded through her—anger at herself because she'd got herself into this mess in the first place, and anger at him because he was so obviously enjoying every minute of it. She clenched her hands together, knowing that she'd like nothing better than to slap that smile off his face, but it was a luxury she couldn't afford. She needed his help whether she liked it or not.

'Could. . .could you give me a hand. . .please?' she said with difficulty.

'Wise decision,' he observed. 'If you'd acted on your first impulse you'd be lying face down in the mud right now.'

'I don't know what you mean,' she said stiffly.

His eyebrows rose and she coloured. 'Look, are you going to help me or not?' she demanded.

'I've two suggestions,' he said. 'You could take off your shoes and walk in your bare feet. You're not wearing stockings, are you?'

'No,' she muttered, all too conscious that his gaze was fixed on her legs. 'And your second suggestion?'

'I could carry you.'

'Certainly not!' she gasped, hot colour flooding into her cheeks.

'It's up to you,' he replied, infuriatingly calm. 'And I'd recommend that you make up your mind quickly—it's going to rain.'

Abby gazed up at the sky. He was right, damn him.

'I'll take my shoes off,' she said, bending down towards one foot and almost toppling over in the process.

'For God's sake, don't do it like that or you will end up flat on your face!' he exclaimed.

'You, of course, have a much better way?' she retorted.

'Lean on my shoulders and I'll get your shoes off,' he said, crouching down in front of her and grasping one of her ankles before she realised what he was doing.

'You're ruining your suit,' she protested shakily, all too aware that the touch of his fingers on her bare skin was sending tiny shivers coursing through her.

'And there was me thinking you'd devised this whole little excursion with exactly that in mind,' he declared, gazing up at her with a wide smile.

A warm glow of attraction spread through her as she stared down into his deep grey eyes and then just as suddenly her heart contracted. Now she knew what it was about him that she found so strangely familiar and unsettling. Michael, she thought wretchedly; he reminds me of Michael.

'Hey, I was only joking,' Sean said quickly, seeing her face whiten. 'Are you OK?'

'I'm fine,' she lied. 'Just. . .just a little cold.'

'Here,' he said, slipping off his jacket and wrapping it round her shoulders before she could protest. 'OK, that's your shoes off. Take my hand and I'll keep you upright.'

She did as he ordered, scarcely aware of him now. She had been so sure that her past was buried, so certain that her memories no longer had the power to hurt her, but all it had taken was one smile to resurrect all the old misery and pain.

'Now, are there any mountains to climb or streams to ford before we reach this cottage of mine?' Sean asked when they finally reached firmer ground.

'It's just up there,' she muttered, pointing to the house ahead and squeezing her mud-caked feet back into her ruined shoes with difficulty.

'So near?' he commented. 'How very disappointing—I was sure we must have a five-mile hike ahead of us at least.'

Despite herself her lips twitched.

'Was that a smile?' he exclaimed. 'Did my eyes deceive me or did I actually see the merest suspicion of a smile just then?'

It was well-nigh impossible to remain aloof when she knew just how dreadful she must look and a small chuckle escaped from her.

'Eureka!' he cried, punching his hand to the sky in triumph. 'The lady does have a sense of humour!'

She started to laugh and he joined her. He had been right on both counts, he thought with satisfaction. Abby Hunter could be a likeable woman when she wanted to be and when she smiled she became quite attractive—in fact rather more than quite attractive, he decided with surprise.

'Look, I don't need a university degree to know you resent my appointment,' he observed. 'Why don't you just say it to my face, get it out in the open, and then we can forget it?'

She eyed him warily. 'Bad idea, Sean—I have to work for you, remember.'

'We're on our own time here, Abby. Forget I'm your chief of staff—speak your mind.'

She hesitated for just a moment. 'OK, then, yes, I do resent you getting the job. I know this place inside out—all your experience has been in large NHS hospitals.'

'I've considerably more administrative experience than you have, Abby.'

'I ran Ardmar for three months after Dr Lawrie died, and I was always left in charge when he went away on holiday or to conferences.'

'That's hardly administrative experience.'

His tone was distinctly disparaging and she bristled instinctively. 'What would you call it, then?' she demanded.

'Well, I'm sure you coped fine with the secretarial jobs. . .'

'The *secretarial* jobs?' she choked. 'Why, you arrogant, chauvinistic. . .I thought George Benson was bad, but not even he has ever had the nerve to come out out with a sexist comment like that!'

A faint tinge of colour appeared on his cheeks. He knew only too well that many male members of the medical profession tolerated women doctors rather than accepted them, but he wasn't a chauvinist— was he?

'All I'm trying to say—probably very badly,' he replied stiffly, 'is that filling in for a few months isn't the same as running an establishment full time, and, while women undoubtedly excel at communication skills, the chief of staff's job calls for other qualities— practical skills which women tend to find more difficult.'

For a second she thought he must be joking, but one glance at his face told her he wasn't. 'What ark did you come out of, for God's sake?' she exclaimed angrily. 'We've had women prime ministers, women heads of state. . .'

'OK, OK, let's not get into a feminist argument,' he replied, beginning to feel distinctly rattled. 'Can't you just concede I was the better all-round candidate?'

On paper she knew he was, and she should have just left it there, but she was too angry for that. 'You're too well qualified, Sean.'

His black brows snapped down. 'What do you mean?'

'I want to know why you came here; why would someone like you even consider coming here?'

A flash of real anger appeared on his face. 'You think I'm indulging in some massive ego trip—that's it, isn't it? That I came here because I want to be a big fish in a little pond?'

She did, but it was amazing how appalling it sounded when it was put into words. 'I didn't mean that. . . You're twisting my words,' she faltered.

He saw the lie in her eyes. 'Lady, I'd say the only thing that's twisted around here is your own bloody ego! So only Abby Hunter has a vocation, does she? Only she could possibly have a desire to serve a community, is that it?'

'No, I didn't mean—'

'Oh, yes, you did,' he interrupted, his voice ice-cold. 'And I tell you this: unless you shape up your ideas pretty damn quick you're shortly going to be looking for new employment!'

'What ever happened to "Forget I'm your chief of staff—speak your mind"?' she protested, her colour high. 'As soon as I ask you a question you don't like I get it in the neck—that's hardly adult behaviour!'

'And you think it's adult behaviour, do you, to take your new chief of staff down a country lane in the hope he'll get stuck in the mud?' he thundered.

She flushed deeply. 'Sean. . . Dr Maguire. . .'

'I'm prepared to excuse your behaviour on this occasion, assume it's due more to premenstrual tension than sheer sour grapes—'

'*Premenstrual tension*!' she exploded. 'Why you, you. . .!' Speechless with rage, she pulled his jacket from her shoulders, handed it to him without a word, and turned on her heel.

'Where do you think you're going?' he demanded.

'Home,' she said crisply. 'As you so rightly pointed out, I'm on my own time now and I can spend it how I choose!'

Dimly she heard him calling after her but she kept on walking. Of all the arrogant, self-opinionated chauvinists she had ever had the misfortune to meet he had to be the worst, she thought savagely. For two pins she would have liked to go back, to give him a cogent and extremely colourful assessment of his character, and then resign on the spot, but there was no way she was going to give him that satisfaction— no way. If anyone should resign it was him and the quicker the better.

He has a lovely smile, a little voice whispered at the back of her head as the heavens suddenly opened and torrential rain began to fall.

'I don't give a damn about his lovely smile!' she shouted to the leaden sky, only to hear the mocking little voice whisper back, 'Liar!'

CHAPTER TWO

'DR HUNTER—Abby—wait up there a minute!'

With a groan, Abby let the door to Ward 1 swing shut again as Sean Maguire strode purposefully down the corridor towards her. She'd spent a sleepless night, all too conscious that no matter what she thought of him privately he was still her boss and if she wanted to stay on at Ardmar—and she did—she was going to have to apologise. She took a deep breath.

'I think I owe you an apology.'

They'd spoken in unison and for a second they stared at one another and then Sean laughed. 'Shall I go first?'

'If you want,' she answered, wondering just how much of what he'd said he was going to apologise for.

'I think we both got a bit heated last night,' he observed. 'Why don't we start afresh this morning, pretend that yesterday never happened?'

It was hardly the most fulsome of apologies, but if they were going to have the remotest chance of being able to work together she supposed she had to accept it.

'I'm game if you are,' she replied.

He held out his hand. 'My name is Sean Maguire and I'm delighted to meet you.'

'And my name is Abby Hunter and I'm pleased to meet you,' she said.

They stood gazing at one another uncertainly for a moment and it was Abby who broke the silence. 'You'll have to excuse me—I've my rounds to start. . .'

'Mind if I come with you—get my bearings?'

'You're the boss,' she replied, only to see his black

24

brows snap down immediately. 'That wasn't intended as a dig, Sean,' she added mildly; 'it was just an automatic response.'

He shook his head and sighed. 'That suggestion of mine to play the truth game was a big mistake. We're going to spend half our time walking on eggshells and the other half apologising to one another.'

'You think it's going to be that difficult for us to get on?' she said.

'I'm hoping not.'

His eyes were fixed on her and she found she could not meet them. What was it about this man that reminded her so much of Michael? she wondered in confusion. The two men weren't even remotely similar in looks. Michael's hair had been fair, not black like Sean's, and his eyes had been brown, not grey.

But then, as a slow smile crept across Sean's face and an answering one was irresistibly drawn from her, she suddenly knew what it was. It was charm. Both men possessed the same immense charm, but she had learned the hard way just how superficial and destructive such a quality could be.

Squaring her shoulders deliberately, she pushed open the swing doors and led the way into the ward.

'Any problems last night, Staff Nurse Johnson?' she asked as Kate handed her the notes the night staff had made.

Silence was her only reply and Abby looked round curiously to find Kate's eyes fixed admiringly on Sean.

'Earth calling Kate Johnson!' she said pointedly. 'Any problems last night with the patients?'

Kate blushed. 'No problems at all, Doctor.'

Abby shook her head. The damn man had only been on the premises a few hours and yet already half the female staff were smitten. By the end of the week she'd be hard-pressed to find anyone who didn't think he was Mr Wonderful. Well looks and charm didn't impress her one bit, she told herself firmly as she began her rounds.

Ardmar boasted only six wards but by the time Abby reached the last one she felt totally wrung out. She'd tried her best to behave normally, to carry out her duties as she usually did, but it had been virtually impossible. Sean had questioned everything—from the treatment that was being given to the treatment that had been administered in the past—until she felt that not only were her own abilities being scrutinised and found wanting, but Ardmar's were too.

'Everything quiet today, Carol?' she asked hopefully as she went into Ward 6 and Carol Lennox came towards her with a welcoming smile.

'John-Robert is being his usual troublesome self,' she replied, 'but other than that everything's fine.'

Quickly Abby checked on the other patients and then came to John-Robert, an expression of mock severity on her face. 'I hear you've been creating mayhem.'

The eight-year-old grinned up at her and then stared down resentfully at his heavily plastered left leg. 'I get bored, Dr Abby.'

'John-Robert has osteopetrosis,' she explained, handing Sean his medical chart. 'It's a rare inherited disease—his osteoclast cells aren't functioning properly so his bone structure isn't as dense as it should be.'

'I do recognise the term,' he said mildly.

She flushed. Of course he did—with her luck he'd probably written a damn book on it.

'Dr Abby means my bones aren't strong enough,' John-Robert declared helpfully. 'I get lots of fractures.'

Sean smiled. 'Boaster! How many is lots?'

'Fifteen—not including the leg,' John-Robert replied proudly.

'A regular disaster area, aren't you?' Sean observed. He glanced at the medical chart. 'I see his osteopetrosis isn't severe. Did you try bone-marrow transplantation when he was younger?'

Abby stiffened. Why did he have to make every question sound like a criticism of the work at Ardmar? 'He had two,' she said evenly, 'but his body rejected both.'

'I'm afraid you're going to be stuck here for another week, John-Robert,' Sean said, turning back to the child. 'Your temperature's gone up a bit so we'll have to keep you in.'

'You talk really funny,' John-Robert commented, gazing up at him with a frown.

'Why, sure and begorra and why would you be thinking that?' Sean said.

John-Robert's frown deepened momentarily and then he chuckled. 'You're daft!'

'John-Robert!' Abby exclaimed in red-cheeked consternation.

'It's OK,' Sean grinned. 'I've been called a lot worse—and quite recently too,' he added, shooting a sly sideways glance at her.

Abby led the way out of the ward, her cheeks pink, and paused in the corridor. 'I'm sure you must have a ton of work waiting for you in your office, Sean, so if there's nothing else. . .?'

'Is that side ward occupied, Staff Nurse Lennox?' he asked, turning to Carol and indicating the door opposite.

Carol gazed at Abby in mute appeal.

'It has one patient—Becky Reid,' Abby said, coming to Carol's rescue quickly. 'But, as I said, I'm sure you must be wanting to get back to your office—'

'I'd like to see the girl,' he interrupted. 'Unless there's some reason I shouldn't?' he added, looking from Abby to Carol thoughtfully.

Abby shrugged at Carol in defeat. She supposed he was bound to find out sooner or later. Quickly, she opened the door and they all filed in.

'What's the problem here?' Sean asked, his gaze taking in the child's blank face and unhappy eyes.

'Becky's broken her back,' Abby replied, smoothing the girl's long blonde hair back from her forehead gently. 'Her father's car was hit by a lorry and she was in the back seat. . .'

'Don't tell me,' he sighed. 'She wasn't wearing a seat belt and went straight through the windscreen?'

Abby nodded. 'Her father had his seat belt on—he walked away with minor abrasions.'

Sean shook his head. 'What a waste. Just a minute,' he added as Abby turned towards the door with relief, 'According to this record she was admitted three months ago and the only treatment she's receiving is physiotherapy. There's no note here of any special medication. Why hasn't she been discharged?'

'A place wasn't available at Norwood,' Abby replied, crossing her fingers behind her back.

'But she doesn't need to go to Norwood!' he exclaimed. 'She's not an orphan. Why can't she go home?'

She debated lying to him but she doubted she'd get away with it—Sean was too smart to be easily deceived. The only thing that would satisfy him was the truth. She cleared her throat. 'Becky's father won't take her home.'

He gazed at her in bewilderment and then at Carol, who suddenly seemed to find the back wall extremely interesting, and a deep frown appeared on his forehead. Without a word he threw open the ward door and strode outside, motioning to them to follow him.

'You can go, Staff Nurse Lennox,' he declared,

waving his hand dismissively at Carol who beat a hasty retreat with a backward glance of sympathy at Abby. 'OK,' he continued as soon as the door to Ward 6 was safely shut, 'I want some straight answers and I want them now, Abby. What do you mean Becky Reid's father won't take her home?'

If the situation hadn't been so serious Abby would have laughed. She felt as though she was back at school, facing her old headmaster over some misdemeanour she had committed, but Sean wasn't her headmaster and she was no longer a child.

'Becky's father won't take her home because he can't face the situation,' she replied. 'He hasn't visited her once since she was admitted. She's not just paraplegic, you see, she's brain damaged too.'

'Then she most definitely shouldn't be here. Ardmar doesn't have the facilities to deal with mental conditions. . .' He came to a halt, his eyes narrowing slightly. 'You knew that when you admitted her, didn't you?'

Her chin came up defiantly. 'I made an administrative decision based on my understanding of the case.'

'A decision that didn't include attempting to persuade her father to accept his responsibility, it would appear,' he retorted. 'She's his daughter, for God's sake!'

'I did try to persuade him,' she protested, 'but Ben's had a really rough time lately. His wife died two years ago and Becky was all he had left. Can you imagine what it must be like to have a beautiful, healthy six-year-old one day and then be faced with a child who will never walk again—a child whose mental age will never progress beyond that of a toddler?'

'So you allowed him to dump her on us, to forget about her?' he replied, tight-lipped.

'I'm hoping that if we don't pressurise him he'll come to terms with the situation. . .'

'A highly unlikely scenario if he never visits, wouldn't you say?' he threw back. 'His telephone number will be in the hospital records, I suppose?'

She gazed at him uncertainly. 'Don't go in at the deep end, Sean. Ben needs careful handling. . .'

'Letting the matter slide as you've been doing sure as heck hasn't achieved very much,' he said grimly. 'I'd say it's high time Mr Reid heard some straight talking.'

'Sean—'

'My decision, Abby,' he broke in. 'Hospital administration is my concern and this is an administrative matter so don't interfere.'

She opened her mouth and then closed it again.

'And while we're on the subject of administrative matters,' he continued, producing a sheet of paper from his pocket, 'this proposal of yours that Ardmar should buy a new minibus for the day centre—I'm not going to sanction it at the next board meeting. We can't afford it, not at the current time.'

She took a deep breath and struggled to remain calm.

'Yes, we can—our current budget is showing an adequate surplus this year.'

'A surplus that I've decided would be better spent on upgrading the waiting room facilities,' he replied. 'They're totally unacceptable at the moment and hardly suggest a modern, forward-thinking hospital to either the patients or to potential benefactors.'

She gritted her teeth. She was not going to lose her temper even if it killed her. 'I'm sure our patients will manage to struggle through another year without the benefits of posh seats, fancy wallpaper and potted plants, whereas a modern minibus would make a huge difference to the day centre—'

'I agree and we'll certainly buy one next year,' he interrupted, 'but this year any budget surplus is going to be spent on the hospital waiting rooms.'

He turned to walk away from her and she caught his arm quickly.

'The minibus—your refusal to OK my proposal— that wouldn't have anything to do with what I said to you yesterday, would it?' she demanded.

His grey eyes flashed. 'Believe it or not, I'm not that petty. My decision is based purely on the priorities as I see them. I've made my decision—and that's my final word on the subject, Abby,' he added as she opened her mouth to protest. 'Now you'll have to excuse me. I'm taking Finlay Norris out to lunch at the Woodside and if I don't hurry I'm going to be late.'

For five seconds she stared after his retreating back, telling herself that she didn't give a damn if he went to hell with Finlay Norris, and then she ran after him.

'Don't take Finlay to the Woodside, Sean,' she said breathlessly. 'It's the most expensive restaurant in town. . .'

'And the cost of the lunch is coming out of my pocket,' he said stiffly, 'so there's no need to imply I'm ripping off the hospital.'

'I wasn't implying that,' she protested. 'It's just that Finlay will think lunch there is a complete waste of money.'

'Finlay Norris is one of our wealthiest supporters,' he said coldly. 'Where do you suggest I take him—to a hamburger stall? He's hardly likely to feel in a very generous frame of mind after that, is he?'

'Will you listen to me?' she cried as he began to walk on. 'This isn't London, this is Ardmar. People here have very fixed ideas. . .'

He whirled round to face her, his face thunderous. 'You just won't accept it, will you? You just won't accept you're not in charge any more. Well, you're not—so don't you dare presume to teach me my job!'

'Oh, don't be so bloody childish!' she retorted, and then bit her lip at the look in his eyes. 'I'm sorry—I shouldn't have said that—but I'm only trying to help you, to give you the benefit of my local knowledge. . .'

'Which when I need it I'll ask for—understood?'

She stared up into his cold face, into his eyes which said all too clearly, Don't ever think you can get the better of me because you can't, and gave up. 'Loud and clear, Dr Maguire; loud and clear.'

She was still standing in the middle of the corridor some minutes later when Dr Bell came out of the X-ray department.

'Something wrong, Abby?' he asked, seeing her deep frown.

She sighed. 'Not yet, there isn't, Alastair, but there sure as heck's going to be.'

'Sorry?' Alastair said in confusion.

'You're not the only one, Alastair,' Abby said ruefully. 'You're not the only one.'

She had little time to wonder how Sean's lunch with Finlay Norris was going. She grabbed a sandwich and a cup of coffee in the hospital canteen and then set to work on the part of her job she liked least—the dispensary supplies. Filling in triple forms might be essential, but she loathed paperwork of any kind, so it was with relief that she finally emerged from the dispensary some two hours later.

Her relief was short-lived. Sean was waiting for her.

'Can I have a word?' he asked.

'I'm on my way to Physiotherapy,' she said curtly.

He looked disappointed. Probably wants to have

another go at me, she thought acidly, but she was
damned if she was going to give him the opportunity.

'I need to talk to you,' he said as she turned
on her heel. 'It won't take long, I promise—and it is
important.'

He didn't look disappointed, she realised. He looked
decidedly uncomfortable.

'What's wrong?' she asked.

He glanced down the corridor. 'Not here. Come to
my office.'

She followed him up the stairs and into his office,
pausing momentarily on the threshold. Even three
months after William Lawrie's death she still couldn't
come into this room without expecting to find him
sitting behind the desk. He had been a crotchety old
devil when he chose but oh, how she missed him,
missed his sudden flashes of humour, his gentle advice.

'Something the matter?' he asked, seeing her
hesitation.

She shook her head deliberately. 'What's this problem that can't wait?'

'Finlay Norris.'

Her eyebrows lifted. 'What about Finlay Norris?'

He picked up a folder from his desk and then put
it down again. 'You were right and I was wrong.'

'The lunch didn't go well?'

'If you can think of a word vastly worse than cata-
strophic you might just about come close,' he sighed.
'We ended up having a take-away while Finlay gave
me an earful on the subject of wasting hospital funds.'

'But didn't you tell him you were paying for the
lunch yourself?' she said.

'I did and he said it was clearly time the board took
a long, hard look at what they were paying me.'

She said nothing and he pulled a hand through his
black hair ruefully. 'Go on, say it. Say "I told you so".'

She shook her head. 'Don't think I'm not tempted, but what's done is done. I presume you didn't persuade him to increase his donation this year?'

He stared down at his hands. 'It's rather worse than that, I'm afraid. He told me he might cancel his contribution altogether.'

'Oh, Sean, no!' she said in horror. 'The hospital can't afford to lose a single donation.'

'Do you think I don't know that?' he protested. 'I was wondering. . .' He came to a halt.

'You were wondering what?' she prompted.

'Finlay seemed to think very highly of you,' he said, a slight tinge of colour appearing on his cheeks. 'I was wondering—could you phone him—try and persuade him to change his mind?'

She frowned. 'Finlay has a very short fuse and when he gets on his high horse it can be one hell of a job to get him down.'

'Crawl if you have to—promise him anything if you have to—but get him to change his mind.'

She reached for the phone and then paused. 'And what do I get out of this if I succeed—apart from the knowledge that I've pulled your butt out of the fire?'

'My eternal gratitude?'

'Too vague.'

'Lunch at a restaurant of your choice—but don't, for God's sake, choose the Woodside!' he added with a grin.

'Tempting, but no, thanks.'

'Dinner—a week's paid leave?'

She shook her head.

'OK, then, what would persuade you?' he demanded.

'Let my proposal for the new minibus go ahead.'

He eyed her speculatively. 'That's blackmail, Abby Hunter.'

'I'd say that was called demonstrating my practical skills, Dr Maguire,' she said sweetly.

A smile spread across his face. 'I asked for that, didn't I? OK, I'll sanction the proposal—but only if you can pull it off.'

Calming Finlay Norris down was hard enough, and making him change his mind took all the guile she possessed, but eventually she managed it so that by the time she rang off he was actually laughing and not only promising to continue his contribution to the hospital but also implying that he might increase it after all.

'I owe you one for that,' Sean said with relief as she replaced the receiver, 'but did you really have to suggest I was a flash city slicker, unused to country ways?'

'I could always phone him back and tell him that in reality you're just too pigheaded to listen to a bit of friendly advice,' she replied, reaching for the phone.

'Not on your life!' he exclaimed, putting his hand over hers quickly. 'He can think I'm the worst form of low life imaginable if it means he won't cancel his donation.'

She withdrew her hand from under his, conscious with acute annoyance that her cheeks were flushing.

'Well, at least I got one thing right,' he observed as she got to her feet hurriedly. 'Women do have good communication skills.'

Her eyebrows rose. 'On this occasion it's just as well, don't you think?'

He chuckled as he opened the door for her. 'You said you were going over to Physiotherapy—mind if I come along, introduce myself to the staff there?'

She minded very much. She hadn't spoken to Robert for a couple of days and the last person she wanted with her when she did so was Sean Maguire, but she could hardly tell him that.

'Fine,' she said tightly, leading the way down the stairs.

'What's wrong?' he asked. 'What have I said now?'

'Do you have to keep checking up on me?' she asked, taking refuge in attack. 'I'm good at my job, Sean. I don't need an overseer.'

'I never thought for one minute you did,' he said in confusion, holding open the swing doors at the bottom of the stairs for her. 'I just want to see everything, and as you told me you know the place inside out I thought you'd be the logical person to shadow. Dr Lawrie must have come on your rounds with you, surely?'

'Yes, but he was—' She pulled herself up short.

'A friend?' he finished for her. 'Can't we be friends, Abby?'

'We might stand a better chance if you didn't bite my head off every time I try to help,' she said, slipping under his arm and out onto the gravel path.

'*Me* bite *your* head off?' he exclaimed. 'You have a temper and a half, my girl, though I guess I should have expected it from the colour of your hair.'

She groaned. 'Has it ever occurred to you that the real reason people with red hair have such tempers is because they get so damn fed up with people saying that to them all the time?'

'Sorry,' he grinned. 'Your hair's beautiful,' he added, reaching out to touch it without warning.

'It's red, certainly,' she replied, pulling away from him sharply and quickening her pace, all too conscious that her heart had skipped a beat.

It would be so easy to like this man, she thought, to more than like him, but a little voice whispered warningly at the back of her mind, No, Abby, not this man; never this man.

'Did you know this hospital used to be Sir Duncan

Munroe's shooting lodge?' she said, deliberately changing the subject.

'So I understand,' he said, eyeing her curiously.

'When his son died from muscular dystrophy he decided to convert the lodge into a children's hospital for the local community.'

She paused to gaze out at the immaculate lawns, the flowerbeds bright with summer colour, and the dark waters of the Moray Firth in the distance.

'We do good work here, Sean, worthwhile work. Because we're small we can supply a more personal touch, a continuity of care that would be impossible in a larger establishment. We never turn anyone away, no matter how hopeless the case might seem, no matter how many other hospitals have said nothing can be done. . .'

She came to a halt, aware that his gaze was no longer curious but intent, and laughed shakily. 'Sorry, but once I start talking about Ardmar I just don't know when to stop.'

'Don't apologise,' he replied. 'It's good to hear such eloquent testimony from someone who has a real love for the place, a real belief in it.'

'I do love it here,' she murmured. 'It would be criminal if it had to close.'

'Which is why I don't intend to let that happen. Look, Abby, what I said to you yesterday about female doctors—and that cheap crack of mine about PMT—I didn't mean it.'

'No?' Her voice revealed her disbelief.

'Well, OK, maybe I did mean the bit about women doctors,' he said ruefully. 'The trouble is the medical profession's still largely a male preserve and I guess I've picked up prejudices and preconceptions without even realising it—though I have to say it came as a bit of a shock to find out I'd become a chauvinist pig.'

'I didn't call you that,' she protested. 'I said you were a chauvinist.'

'There's a difference?'

She chuckled. 'A subtle one certainly—but there is a difference.'

'Thank God for that,' he grinned. 'You think I can be cured, then?'

'It depends upon whether you want to be,' she smiled.

'I know I need your help—my lunch with Finlay Norris proved that beyond doubt,' he said. 'The hospital's in a hell of a bad way, Abby. The funds Sir Duncan invested haven't been bringing in good returns and we're scarcely keeping our heads above water.'

'I'll help all I can—you know that, don't you?' she said quickly.

'I'm counting on it,' he smiled.

Robert was working out a programme of exercise for one of their muscular dystrophy patients when they arrived in the physiotherapy department, but he stopped as soon as he saw them.

'Robert, this is our new chief of staff,' Abby declared. 'Sean, meet Robert Forrest—one of the best physios in the business.'

'Flatterer,' Robert grinned, thrusting a hand through his already tousled brown hair, his open, frank face showing his pleasure. 'Is this a social call or business?'

'Sean wanted to see the department and I wanted a word about Archie Graham—the cystic fibrosis case I'm sending down to you tomorrow.'

'I gather Archie thinks physiotherapy's a waste of time?' he said.

'His parents are carrying out postural drainage at home, and his GP has prescribed pancreatic enzyme tablets and vitamins, but he's really depressed, Robert, so he's going to need a lot of morale-boosting. I'd suggest—'

'Who's the physio here?' he exclaimed. 'I know what I'm doing, Abby.'

She coloured, well aware of Sean's presence.

'I wasn't implying you didn't, Robert.'

'There's a novelty,' he declared, his eyebrows rising comically. 'This woman would run every department in the hospital if she could, Sean.'

'So I've found out,' he chuckled.

'Hey, what's this—gang up on Abby Hunter day?' she protested.

'No offence meant, sweetheart,' Robert smiled, slipping his arm around her waist and drawing her close.

Conscious of Sean's gaze, she eased herself free, suddenly embarrassed, though she did not know why.

'I've got tickets for that concert you wanted to see at the Eden Court in Inverness,' Robert continued. 'I thought we could take in a meal first—'

'I'll talk to you about it later, Robert,' she said quickly. 'Now you'll have to excuse me. Perhaps you'd like to stay, Sean—have a detailed look around?'

'Another time. I've seen all I want to for the present.'

She glanced up at him sharply, almost certain that he wasn't referring simply to the physiotherapy department, but his face was totally bland.

'Come back any time,' Robert said. 'I'm told I make a mean cup of coffee.'

'I'll remember that,' Sean replied, leading the way towards the door.

The weather had changed in the brief time they'd spent in Physiotherapy and as they emerged into the open air Abby pulled her white coat closer to her with a shiver, feeling a chill wind blowing off the Moray Firth.

'So that was your fiancé—Robert Forrest?'

There was something in Sean's voice—something almost like disbelief tinged with a touch of amusement—that had her hackles rising instinctively.

'It was,' she said deliberately.

'Interesting.'

She waited, certain that he was going to add something else, but when he didn't she couldn't contain herself. 'Is that remark supposed to mean something?' she demanded, unaccountably ruffled.

'Nothing at all,' he replied mildly.

'Robert is an excellent physiotherapist.'

'I'm sure he is.'

'He's a kind and considerate man.'

'I don't recall saying he wasn't.'

She gazed at him impotently. It was none of his business whom she chose to marry, so why was she letting it get under her skin? And it really was getting under her skin—she knew it was.

'Molly Jordan told me you and Robert have been engaged for two years,' he observed.

Abby's lips tightened. Not for nothing was Sean's secretary known as the Ardmar Bugle.

'She said you haven't set the wedding day yet,' he continued.

'Molly would appear to have far too damn much to say for herself,' she replied tartly.

'Oh, she's a mine of information,' he said evenly. 'She even told me you have a cottage in the grounds of Ardmar like me, but Robert lives in a flat in town.'

'Does this conversation actually have some point to it?' she demanded.

'I was just wondering which of you had the iron self-control—you or Robert.'

Hot crimson colour flooded through her cheeks. 'My private life is none of your damn business, Sean!'

'I'm sorry—have I touched a raw nerve?' he asked,

his face penitent, although she noticed that his eyes
were gleaming.

'Certainly not,' she snapped. 'I just don't like being
interrogated, that's all.'

One eyebrow rose. 'I wouldn't call asking if Robert
Forrest is your fiancée interrogating you.'

That wasn't what had upset her and he knew it. It
was his clear curiosity as to why she and Robert hadn't
set a wedding date and why they didn't live together.
And she had no intention of revealing that the
decisions had been hers, not Robert's.

'Look, if I've upset you I can assure you it wasn't
intentional,' he continued.

Like hell it wasn't, she thought. 'As you appear to
know so much about my private life, Sean—'

'Not the really interesting bits, unfortunately,' he
broke in, a wicked grin playing about his lips.

'As you appear to know so much about my private
life,' she continued determinedly, 'how about I ask you
a few personal questions?'

'Fire away,' he replied with a smile.

'You're thirty-six and, according to your CV, single.'

'You were interested enough to read it? I'm
flattered.'

'Don't be,' she retorted. 'I was only interested in
your qualifications.'

'I'm crushed,' he sighed.

'Was your CV correct?' she continued, ignoring his
crestfallen expression. 'You're thirty-six and single?'

'Correct on both counts.'

'You've never married?'

'I've made a great many mistakes in my life, but
that isn't one of them.'

'You think being married is a mistake?' she said in
genuine surprise.

'For me it would be,' he replied. 'I'm not the marrying kind.'

Her lip curled unconsciously. 'That, if you don't mind me saying so, is a politely euphemistic way of saying you enjoy playing the field too much to want to give it up and face shouldering some responsibilities.'

'And that, if you don't mind *me* saying so, sounds very much like the voice of experience talking,' he observed. 'And as Robert Forrest doesn't strike me as the kind of man to play around just who, exactly, are you comparing me to?'

She coloured. She had said too much—way too much. Her memories were her own private misery and no one was ever going to know the truth about her and Michael, about the humiliation he'd put her through. She had her pride left, if nothing else.

'I didn't mean anyone,' she said rapidly. 'It was just a general observation, that's all. And now you'll have to excuse me—I'm going to be late for my evening rounds.'

'Abby, wait. . .'

But she was already running along the gravel path, her white coat flapping round her slim legs, her red hair streaming in the wind like a banner. He stared after her for a moment, a slight frown on his forehead. She was a strange one, this Abby Hunter—a spitting hell-cat one moment, a shuttered enigma the next. Well, he'd always liked a challenge, he decided with a grin, and finding out what made Abby Hunter tick was certainly going to be one hell of a challenge.

CHAPTER THREE

'ROSIE DONALDSON, if you don't stop bursting those balloons right this minute I'm going to leave you behind at the day centre!' Abby declared.

Rosie's face crumpled but her large brown eyes sparkled mischievously. 'Sorry, Dr Abby.'

Not half as sorry as I am, Abby thought as she pushed her damp hair back from her forehead wearily. On days like this she knew she must be mad. Anyone who voluntarily took ten lively disabled youngsters out for the day—ten lively youngsters ranging in age from eight to fourteen—knowing that if there wasn't a row on the outward journey there would undoubtedly be one on the way back just had to be certifiable.

She glanced at her watch with irritation. Robert was late. The lifting gear on the brand-new minibus had ensured that all the children were safely on board, and her medical bag was stowed under the front seat in case of an emergency, but still there was no sign of him.

'If Robert's going to be much longer I really think we should take the children off the bus,' Carol observed. 'It's so hot, Abby.'

It was and, judging by the cloudless blue sky, it was going to get even hotter.

'I'm really grateful to you for volunteering to come with us on your day off, Carol,' she said.

'No sweat,' the girl replied, and then chuckled as Abby grimaced expressively. 'Sorry, that was a rather unfortunate observation on a day like this, wasn't it?'

'And how,' Abby laughed, wishing she'd opted to wear shorts like Carol rather than her blue sundress with its fitted bodice and wide straps. 'There you are, Robert!' she declared with relief as he appeared on the steps of the main building looking distinctly harassed. 'We'd just about given you up.'

'I'm afraid I'm going to have to cry off, Abby,' he said.

'But you promised, Robert,' she protested. 'The kids have been looking forward to this trip all week and I can't go without another qualified driver.'

'I really am sorry,' he replied uncomfortably, 'but I completely forgot I'd booked Jamie Brownlie in for the start of his treatment today.'

A silence fell over the minibus and Abby knew that ten pairs of anxious eyes were gazing imploringly at her through the windows. She sighed. No matter how disappointed the kids were going to be, the trip would have to be cancelled. The chances were that nothing would go wrong, but there was always that possibility and she just couldn't take the risk.

She turned towards the minibus, prepared for the inevitable tears and tantrums. 'Sorry, kids, but it looks like the trip's off—'

'No, it isn't,' Sean declared, appearing without warning from behind the minibus. 'I'll come with you.'

Abby groaned as a loud cheer went up from the children. That was all she needed. Sean Maguire was unsettling enough within the confines of the hospital without her being stuck with him all day with absolutely no escape route at all.

'You're not really dressed for a day out,' she said desperately, her eyes taking in his smart dark grey suit, pristine white shirt and red silk tie. 'We're late already and if we wait until you change it will hardly be worth our while going at all.'

'Then I'll go as I am,' he replied. He saw her hesitation and a glimmer of a smile appeared at his lips.

'Considering I was instrumental in the day centre getting this minibus in the first place, it seems only fitting that I should travel on its inaugural trip, don't you think?'

'I guess so,' she said through gritted teeth.

'OK, then, let's get this show on the road,' he said, climbing into the driver's seat.

'I really am sorry, Abby,' Robert murmured, drawing her to one side. 'I'll make it up to you, I promise.'

'How, Robert?' she said in an acid undertone. 'Just how are you going to make it up to me? This was supposed to be a day out for you and me as well as for the kids and now I'm going to be stuck all day with Sean!'

'I didn't do it intentionally, sweetheart,' he replied, his eyes begging for understanding. 'If I could cancel Jamie's appointment I would, but he's been waiting for this treatment for a month already.'

'I just wish you'd remember to keep your appointment book up to date and then things like this wouldn't happen,' she sighed.

'I'll make it up to you,' he said insistently.

She shook her head. 'That's going to take some doing, I can assure you!'

He smiled and bent his head to kiss her and the minibus's horn sounded insistently.

'His Highness is getting impatient,' she said ruefully, extricating herself from his arms. 'See you later, Robert.'

Quickly she walked to the minibus and climbed in beside Sean.

'I thought you said we were late?' he said, revving the engine with quite unnecessary vigour.

'Well, we're all ready now, aren't we?' she replied mildly, wondering why on earth he should suddenly seem so irritated.

He didn't answer and as they set off down the drive Abby glanced over her shoulder at Carol, hoping for some sympathy, but Carol wasn't looking at her. She was gazing back at Ardmar, clear disappointment in her eyes. Sean was in the sulks and Carol was in the doldrums. This was going to be a real fun day out and no mistake!

'Right, where are we off to?' Sean asked when they reached the bottom of the drive.

'Cawdor Castle!' chorused ten small voices.

'Cawdor Castle it is,' he echoed, and shot a swift grin across at Abby who sighed with relief. Whatever had bugged him had clearly been forgotten. Now all she had to do was cheer up Carol.

As it turned out she didn't have to do anything. The combination of ten childish voices and one deep baritone singing 'Ten Green Bottles', 'Old MacDonald Had a Farm', and a decidedly revolting song entitled 'I Want to be Sick' at full pitch soon had Carol laughing with the rest of them.

'I hope you're not regretting your offer to come with us, Carol?' Abby said in an undertone during a temporary lull in the singing.

'Of course not—why?' she answered.

'I just thought you seemed a bit down when we first set off.'

A slight flush of colour appeared on Carol's cheeks. 'It just seemed such a pity Robert couldn't come with us,' she said. 'He works so hard—he could have done with a break.'

'Save your sympathy for us,' Abby laughed. 'Robert's the lucky one—he got to stay behind at the hospital!'

Carol smiled but her colour, Abby noticed, deepened even more.

'Can we sing "I Want to be Sick" again?' Wendy

Wilson asked eagerly before Abby could question Carol further.

'I think we've all heard that particular song quite often enough, thank you,' Abby declared firmly. 'Who on earth started it anyway?'

'Dr Sean!' came the chorus and she gazed at him severely.

'Sorry,' he said, shamefaced, but with laughter plain in his eyes. 'It's a favourite of my nieces and nephews.'

'How many do you have?' she asked with interest.

'Fifteen.'

'*Fifteen*?' she exclaimed. 'Good grief—how many brothers and sisters do you have?'

'No brothers—just five sisters.'

'Poor you,' she laughed. 'That must have driven you mad when you were growing up—one lone man amongst so many women.'

He shook his head. 'It didn't, but then I like women.'

Oh, I'll just bet you do, she thought, but made no comment.

'How many brothers and sisters do *you* have?' he asked, easing the minibus out into the fast lane to overtake a slow-moving tractor.

'None. My parents were killed in a car crash when I was four and an aunt and uncle who had no children of their own took me in.'

'I bet they spoilt you rotten,' he grinned.

'Then you'd lose your money,' she said tightly.

'Dr Abby, we're here, we're here!' Wendy exclaimed excitedly. 'That's the sign, isn't it—C-A-W-D-O-R,' she spelt out carefully.

'Yes, we're here,' Abby laughed, the bleakness in her voice disappearing.

Sean glanced across at her swiftly and then back to the road with a slight frown. Even when Abby's face was alive with laughter he noticed the shadows at the back of her eyes. Something had caused them, something that had gone so deep it was always half-remembered. The frown on his face deepened. There was so much he didn't know about this woman, so much he wanted to know—though he couldn't begin to understand why.

'Will we see where Macbeth murdered Duncan?' Rosie Donaldson demanded, her brown eyes sparkling. 'Will the bloodstains still be on the floor?'

'I'm afraid Cawdor Castle wasn't even built when Macbeth murdered Duncan,' Abby said apologetically. 'Shakespeare just used the castle as an imaginary setting for the deed.'

A chorus of disappointment sounded from behind her.

'I'm sure there were lots of other murders at Cawdor,' Sean said cheerfully as he swung the minibus into the already crowded car park. 'In fact I wouldn't be at all surprised if the entire castle was awash with secretly buried human remains.'

Shrieks of mock horror came from the back of the bus.

'You're going to give them nightmares!' Abby protested.

'This load of little ghouls?' he exclaimed. 'No way!'

It didn't take long to get the children off the bus—their eagerness saw to that.

'How much of the castle can the kids actually see?' Sean asked, slipping off his jacket and unknotting his tie before throwing both over the driver's seat with scant attention to their fineness.

'Those who are in wheelchairs will only be able to visit the ground floor, I'm afraid,' she replied, 'but the gardens are extensive and the gift shop and tea room have ramps so they shouldn't present a problem.'

'There's a duck pond too, you said,' Christopher

Paterson declared, tugging at her dress insistently, a flicker of worry appearing momentarily on his thin face. 'You did say there was a duck pond, didn't you?'

'Yes, I did,' she reassured him. 'And you'll see it, I promise.'

His small face lit up and her throat contracted. Though she knew she shouldn't have favourites, Christopher had held a very special place in her heart from the first day she'd met him. He was such a bright and intelligent eight-year-old, but his cerebral palsy made his speech difficult to understand and because his body jerked and twitched involuntarily the public at large labelled him as retarded. Over Christopher's head her eyes met Sean's sympathetic ones and she smiled tremulously.

It was finally decided, after some squabbling, that Carol would take those children who could walk unaided on a tour of the castle, while the others in wheelchairs or with walking difficulties would stay with Abby and Sean.

'There's no point in going in if we can only see the ground floor,' Craig Lattimer said belligerently, easing his wheelchair onto the gravel path leading to the gardens.

'It's not really the owner's fault,' Sean observed. 'That old castle would probably fall down if they tried to put in elevators.'

'But it's not just here!' Craig exclaimed. 'When my mum takes me to the shops I have to sit outside like I'm a dog or something because my wheelchair won't get in the door. Anyone would think I had leprosy instead of muscular dystrophy.'

Abby gazed at Sean, her expression saying all too clearly, Get out of that one if you can.

'One day you'll be able to get into places like everyone else,' Sean said firmly. 'One day the people who run this country will realise just how important you are and make sure you can get into places.'

Craig grinned up at him. 'Comes the revolution, eh, Doc?'

'Comes the revolution, Craig,' he smiled back.

'You're good with children,' Abby murmured, falling into step beside him as the children went on ahead. 'You should have some of your own.'

'I could say the same about you,' he returned, rolling up the sleeves of his shirt and unbuttoning it almost to the waist.

'We're not talking about me—we're talking about you,' she said hastily, all too conscious of the muscular expanse of chest he had exposed.

'I take my nieces and nephews out on day trips whenever I'm in Ireland. . .'

'That's called having your cake and eating it,' she protested. 'You get all of the perks and none of the drawbacks.'

'I knew there was an advantage in it somewhere,' he said thoughtfully.

She shook her head. 'Aren't you ever serious, Sean Maguire?'

'Oh, when I'm being serious, Abby Hunter, you'll be the first to know it,' he said softly, his eyes gleaming.

She looked away quickly, her cheeks flooding with sudden colour. He was only flirting with her, she knew that, but why couldn't he go and flirt with any one of the dozen nurses at Ardmar who thought he was wonderful? They would enjoy it whereas she. . . What did she feel? Uneasy, uncomfortable, that's how I feel, she thought with annoyance.

When she was with Robert it was different. With Robert she didn't feel on edge and uncertain, she felt in control, but with the man at her side she was only too aware that she was in control of nothing.

'A penny for them?'

'What?' she said uncertainly, glancing up at him.

'A penny for those thoughts that are making you frown.'

'They're not worth it,' she said, her voice deliberately brisk.

'Why don't we sit down, enjoy the sunshine?' he asked, pointing to a seat nearby.

'The children. . .'

'Will come to no harm,' he assured her. 'This garden's completely enclosed and to get out they'd have to pass us. Let them have a little freedom—they'll enjoy it.'

She hesitated for just a moment and then joined him on the seat.

It was a beautiful garden—or, in reality, several small gardens reached through tall pergolas over which honeysuckle and roses scrambled and vied with one another to impress. Each garden possessed a particular style and character of its own. Some were filled with dozens of sweetly scented roses, others had banks of lavender and borders full of old cottage-garden plants, while still more were crowded with montbretia and heather plants that would bloom later in the year.

'It's lovely here,' she murmured, holding her face up to the sun even though she knew she was only inviting another crop of freckles.

'You should get out more,' he observed. 'From what I hear you virtually eat, drink and sleep Ardmar.'

She kept her eyes closed, conscious of the criticism in his voice. 'Ever heard of dedication?' she said defensively.

'Ever heard of a social life?' he countered.

She said nothing. It was none of his damn business how she lived her life.

'Why was your childhood so unhappy?'

She opened her eyes quickly, surprised both at the change in the conversation and the fact that he'd guessed so accurately from the little she'd said. For a moment she didn't reply and then she sighed.

'My aunt and uncle were childless by choice. They didn't want to take me in after my parents were killed but the neighbours would have talked if they'd stuck me in an orphanage. They didn't maltreat me or anything,' she added quickly as a frown appeared on his face. 'I always got enough to eat.'

'Lack of affection can be just as devastating as physical deprivation,' he commented.

Her eyes darkened. 'I tried so hard to please them, Sean, but nothing I ever did was good enough; nothing I ever achieved made them love me. At the end of the day I was just that freckle-faced kid with the red hair they'd got stuck with.'

'Is that why you opted to work with children— because you were unhappy as a child yourself?'

She nodded. 'I knew what it felt like to be frightened and bewildered and so very, very lonely.'

'Oh, my dear,' he murmured, catching her hand in his, his voice gentle.

'Hey, I'm a big girl now,' she said brightly, getting to her feet quickly only to sit down again with a sudden yelp of pain as she felt a sharp tug at the back of her head.

'Don't move,' he ordered. 'Your hair's got caught on the rose bush behind us.'

She didn't move; she couldn't move. With his arms on either side of her head she was virtually pinned to the seat. Carefully he began to disentangle her hair, his face a study in concentration, but while he was totally absorbed in his task she, by contrast, was only conscious of his nearness. Irresistibly her eyes were drawn to the hard muscle of his forearms, to the tiny beads of sweat glistening on his broad chest.

Not a leaf shivered in the hot stillness but she could feel the faint caress of his breath against her cheek, could smell the sharp tang of his aftershave in her nostrils. He had caught his bottom lip between his teeth as he concentrated on a particularly stubborn tangle and, albeit unwillingly, she found herself wondering what it would be like to kiss that mouth, to feel its moist softness against hers, to have those arms that were on either side of her holding her tighter, and to have that body that was so close to hers pressed closer, closer still.

'Am I hurting you?' he said as she shifted slightly on the seat.

'No,' she said, her voice scarcely audible. The stone seat was cool behind her back and yet her body felt on fire, as though every nerve-ending was more sensitive, more acute, than it had ever been before.

'All done,' he said, looking at her at last.

'Thanks,' she murmured with relief, but he did not sit back in his seat.

Instead he slowly, oh, so slowly, traced the contours of her face with his fingertips, his touch so light that it was scarcely more than a summer breeze. In the distance she could hear the children calling to one another, was conscious of the insistent drone of the bees as they flitted from flower to flower, but all she was really aware of was the quizzical look in his grey eyes as he gazed at her, the warmth of his body against hers.

Her heart fluttered and jumped against her throat as he tilted his head towards hers. He was going to kiss her. She knew without a shadow of a doubt that he was going to kiss her—and she knew that if he did she would be lost.

'We'd better round up the kids—they must be

getting hungry by now,' she said, getting to her feet hurriedly.

'Why are you running away?' he asked, puzzlement clear in his face.

'I'm not running away,' she said. 'This trip is for the kids, not for—not for. . .'

'Us to enjoy ourselves?' he suggested, his lips curving into a smile.

Her face set. 'I think we'd better get one thing straight right now, Sean. I don't play games.'

'Games?' he repeated.

'You know very well what I mean.'

'Ah—Robert,' he said slowly.

That hadn't been what she'd meant at all. She hadn't even thought of Robert, but she nodded.

'He isn't right for you, you know,' he observed.

Anger flared within her. 'And you'd know that, would you? On the strength of knowing Robert and me for how long—a month—you'd know that?'

'I'm more experienced than you are. . .'

'Oh, I don't doubt that for a moment,' she said deliberately.

A flash of irritation appeared on his dark face. 'You're doing it again, aren't you—comparing me to someone else?'

She tried to turn away, but he caught her arm and pulled her round to face him.

'Whoever he was, he must have put you through hell,' he said gently, his eyes fixed on her with infinite compassion.

She took a ragged breath, blinking back the tears she knew were threatening to overflow. 'It was a long time ago.'

He sighed. 'Not long enough, it would seem. Abby. . .'

He didn't get the chance to finish what he'd been

about to say. They were suddenly engulfed by four excited children, all determined to speak at once.

'Dr Abby, Dr Abby, we saw a stuffed goat that died after eating a gallon of paint, and there was a tree— a *real* tree—right inside the castle!'

'And there was a fireplace, Dr Sean—a fireplace that was so heavy that when they were carrying it over the drawbridge the drawbridge fell down. . .'

'And there was a dungeon—a proper dungeon— where people were left to starve and everything!'

Abby gazed round at the children's flushed faces and laughed. 'You had a good time, I take it?'

'It was great!' came the reply.

'No problems, Carol?' she asked, her eyebrows raised questioningly.

'The only problem was trying to keep up with this lot,' she replied ruefully. 'How was your group?'

'We were just going to round them up for lunch.'

'But you said we'd see the duck pond,' Christopher exclaimed. 'You did say that; you did promise.'

She glanced down at her watch while Christopher stared at her anxiously. 'All right,' she smiled. 'The duck pond and then lunch.'

It wasn't a large duck pond but Abby doubted whether Disneyland itself could have delighted Christopher more.

'They're so beautiful,' he whispered in awe. 'All those soft white feathers and their yellow beaks— they're so beautiful, aren't they, Dr Abby?'

She nodded.

'One's got a funny walk,' he observed with a slight frown.

'Perhaps it had an accident,' she replied, 'or it might have been born like that.'

'You mean he could be disabled like me?'

Her throat tightened. 'Yes, he could be disabled like you.'

'I hope some of the other ducks are his friends,' Christopher said slowly. 'Sometimes, when you're not like everybody else, people. . .people think you're a freak and they don't want to be friends.'

She gazed at Sean in desperation.

'I'm sure he has lots of friends,' he said firmly. 'He's probably such a nice duck that all the other ducks queue up to be friends with him.'

'I'm hungry!' Wendy protested. 'My tummy's so empty it's making noises.'

'Why don't we go on to Cladach instead of staying at Cawdor?' Abby said quickly. 'It's only ten miles up the road and there's a restaurant where we can sit outside and have our lunch—much nicer than being stuck indoors on such a hot day, don't you think?'

Her suggestion met with a chorus of approval and she sighed with relief. Somehow she didn't want to stay at Cawdor any more.

It didn't take long to reach the restaurant and, though quite a few people had elected to take their meal outside under the collection of brightly coloured umbrellas, they soon found two tables which could accommodate them all and had just finished consulting the menu when the waitress appeared, notebook in hand.

'Ham salad and coffee for me, please,' Abby declared. 'What about you, Sean?'

'The same.'

'Carol?'

'Chicken salad and tea would be great.'

'Right, you ravenous horde—what do you want?' Abby asked, turning to the children.

'Hamburgers and chips!'

'In this weather?' she protested. Ten faces fell quite

ludicrously and she shook her head. 'All right, ten hamburgers and chips it is. And to drink?'

'Milk shakes!' came the chorus.

The waitress's pen hovered uncertainly over her notebook and she turned to Sean. 'What kind of milk shakes do they want?'

'Why don't you ask them?' he smiled.

A slight tinge of colour appeared on the woman's plump face. 'Ask them?' she repeated. 'But they're not. . .I mean they can't. . .' Her voice trailed away into silence.

The smile on Sean's face died. 'They're not what?' he said with deadly politeness.

The waitress flapped her hands helplessly. 'Well, aren't they. . .? They must be. . .oh, you know what I mean.'

'Unfortunately I rather think I do,' he said, his expression hardening, 'but I can assure you the children are perfectly capable of telling you what kind of milk shake they want—unless you have a problem with that?'

The waitress's eyes fell before his and quickly she took the children's orders.

Abby gazed at Sean thoughtfully. Michael wouldn't have said that. Michael wouldn't have been sitting there in the first place, she thought ruefully. Gifted doctor though he was, caring doctor though he was, Michael had always been uncomfortable in the presence of disability and had never understood her interest in this branch of medicine. His skills lay in the operating theatre where he could view patients simply as a collection of malfunctioning organs upon which he could demonstrate his ability.

The food was excellent and the children pronounced the milk shakes wonderful, and Abby was just congratulating herself on her decision not to stay at

Cawdor when she became aware that Christopher kept turning round in his seat.

'What's the matter, Christopher?' she asked. 'Are you too hot where you are?'

'I'm not too hot,' Christopher replied with irritation. 'I just wish everyone wouldn't keep staring at us.'

He was right—people were staring. Abby had noticed it but had hoped the children had not.

'I imagine everyone's just trying to work out how Dr Abby and I managed to have quite so many children,' Sean grinned, winking across at her.

'But we couldn't all be yours,' Will Hardy protested.

'I'm rather afraid you could,' Sean replied ruefully.

Will stared at him in awe. 'Are you really that old?'

'Every bit that old,' Sean declared, his voice mock-quavery.

'But Dr Abby isn't—is she?' Wendy said, staring at her critically.

'Not quite,' Sean answered. 'I would say she could only be the mother of about half of you.'

'Thanks a million!' Abby laughed. 'The only way I could have managed that would have been if you'd kept me permanently pregnant!'

'I can think of worse ways of spending my time,' he said, his eyes dancing, and with acute annoyance Abby felt herself blushing.

'That's not why they're staring at us,' Craig muttered into his milk shake. 'They're staring at us because they think we're freaks and retards.'

A silence descended on the group and Abby bit her lip. It was true. No matter where they went they always aroused this reaction. A few people were deliberately cruel but the majority were simply ignorant, believing that if a child was in a wheelchair or had some physical disability it automatically meant that he or she was mentally impaired as well.

They did not stay long at the restaurant after that. Some of the happiness and the sunshine seemed to have gone out of the day and it was a much quieter group of children who arrived back at Ardmar later that afternoon.

'I had a lovely time,' Christopher declared stoutly as Abby helped him off the bus.

'Good,' she replied.

'And Dr Sean said he'd take me back to Cawdor all by myself if there weren't any more trips planned there for a while,' he continued.

'Did he?'

'And he said not to bother about silly people because they're just too ignorant to know any better.'

'He's right, Christopher.'

'Would you come—with Dr Sean—when we go back to Cawdor?' he demanded.

'We'll see,' she said evasively.

He frowned. 'That's not a promise.'

'Your mum and dad are waiting for you,' she said quickly, waving to the couple waiting expectantly beside their car.

'Promise,' Christopher said insistently. 'Promise you'll come with me and Dr Sean—you're my two most favourite people—next to Mum and Dad of course.'

She stared down into the small, earnest face, a hard lump in her throat, and smiled. 'I promise.'

Suddenly she was very tired and it was with relief that she followed Sean back into the hospital.

'I think the day went off pretty well, considering,' he declared as he followed her up the stairs.

'Apart from Cladach,' she sighed. 'We should have stayed at Cawdor—or, better still, taken a picnic lunch with us.'

'It wasn't your fault,' Sean said as he led the way into his office. 'The general public see disabled people so infrequently, they don't know how to react—they either spend the whole time studiously ignoring them or staring.'

'But it makes me so mad!' she exclaimed. 'If they would only talk to the children they'd find out they're no different from so-called "normal" children.'

'You can't change people's attitudes overnight, I'm afraid,' he replied. 'It takes time, understanding—but it will come, believe me.'

'I hope so,' she declared. 'And now I'd better be off,' she added, holding out the keys to the minibus to him. 'It's been a long day.'

He took the keys from her outstretched hand and then, suddenly and completely without warning, pulled her into his arms and kissed her. His action was so unexpected that she didn't even have time to protest, far less struggle. All she was aware of was his strength, of the hard muscles of his arms around her, of the overwhelming shudders of pleasure flooding through her as he deepened the kiss, parting her lips to explore her mouth with his tongue.

It was only when his lips traced slowly down her throat, when he ran his tongue gently along the line of material covering her breasts and her body convulsed in response, that reality hit her and she jerked herself free of his arms.

'What—what the hell do you think you're doing?' she spluttered, uncomfortably aware that she hadn't wanted the kiss to stop, hadn't wanted the feelings he was arousing in her to end. 'What—why did you do that?'

'Because I've been wanting to all day,' he said, a warm smile creasing his face.

'Then I hope you weren't too disappointed,' she said crisply.

'It wasn't bad for a first attempt but next time will be better, I expect.'

'*Next* time!' she exploded. 'There will be no next time, mister!'

'Why not?' he grinned. 'Didn't you like it?'

'No, I did not!' she retorted.

'Liar.'

'Dr Maguire—'

'The name's Sean, remember?'

'Dr Maguire,' she continued dangerously, 'surprising though it may seem, it is not customary in this hospital for the chief of staff to leap upon members of the female staff!'

'Oh, come on, I hardly leapt on you,' he protested. 'All I did was put my arms around you and kiss you. I can give you another demonstration if you like,' he added, moving towards her.

'Certainly not!' she gasped, strategically putting the desk between them, only to see his smile deepen maddeningly.

'Does Robert kiss you like that?' he asked.

He didn't. Robert had never made her feel the way this man had when he'd kissed her. She felt safe with Robert, but with Sean she didn't feel safe at all and it wasn't a feeling she liked.

'What Robert does or doesn't do is none of your damn business!' she threw back at him.

'I didn't think he did,' he said, his eyes dancing.

She glared at him furiously and then strode deliberately towards the door. 'I've only got one thing to say to you, Sean Maguire.'

'And what's that?'

'Go to hell!' she exclaimed, and banged out of the door, the sound of his laughter echoing behind her.

CHAPTER FOUR

ABBY's colour was high, her brown eyes flashing fire, as she paced her office floor.

'Just who the hell does he think he is, Jean? Just where does he get off with giving me advice? If I wanted to marry Genghis Khan it would be none of his damn business!'

Jean shifted slightly in her seat, her expression a mixture of puzzlement and confusion. 'I can understand you being annoyed, my dear—'

'*Annoyed*! I'm not annoyed, Jean, I'm bloody livid! The conceit of the man—the sheer unadulterated conceit! He seems to think he can ride roughshod over everyone—well, he can't, not with me!'

'Then tell him so.'

'Do you think I haven't tried?' Abby protested. 'But telling him to butt out of my life is like telling him to stop breathing!'

'So ignore him,' Jean declared. 'Don't let him get under your skin like this. I've seen you do it with other men—why can't you do it with him?'

'Because other men haven't—' Abby stopped short, the colour on her cheeks deepening.

'Other men haven't what, my dear?' Jean prompted.

Abby opened her mouth, closed it again, and then could contain herself no longer. 'He kissed me, Jean—he had the unmitigated gall to kiss me!'

Jean gazed at her in open-mouthed astonishment and then leant forward in her seat, her eyes gleaming. 'Was he any good?'

'*Jean*!'

'Sorry,' she said contritely. 'That's not the point, is it? A chief of staff shouldn't behave like that.'

'No, he shouldn't,' Abby declared, uncomfortably recalling that Sean's kiss had been considerably better than just good.

Jean adjusted the jacket of her smart blue suit and smoothed down the folds of her fine silk blouse. 'You know, I'm beginning to wonder if we didn't perhaps make a mistake when we appointed him,' she said, her brown eyes darting swiftly across at Abby and then away again. 'All those qualifications of his—well, they don't necessarily mean he's the right person for the job, do they?'

Abby longed to agree with her but knew in all conscience that she couldn't. 'He's excellent with the children,' she said grudgingly, 'and medically I can't fault him. When Simon Watson went into cardiac arrest last weekend his resuscitation technique was excellent.'

'You could have done just as well, my dear.'

'Yes, but there are other things a chief of staff has to do well—things like the paperwork and the fund-raising. I hate all that but he's good at it.'

'Hold up there a minute,' Jean exclaimed. 'Are we still talking about the same man here—the man you as good as called an arrogant, interfering so-and-so? Sounds to me like you think he's pretty wonderful.'

'All I'm saying is he's good at his job—and don't look at me like that,' Abby added quickly as Jean's lips curved into a knowing smile. 'Personally I think he's an arrogant jerk but professionally I can't fault him.'

Abby's office door swung open and both women jumped guiltily as Sean entered.

'Am I interrupting something?' he asked, pausing in mid-stride.

'Haven't you ever heard of knocking?' Abby

retorted sharply, wondering just how much of their conversation he could possibly have heard through the closed door.

'Sorry,' he replied, though he didn't look in the least penitent. 'No, don't go, Jean,' he added as she got to her feet. 'I've some cheques I need countersigned in my office if you've time.'

She nodded. 'Thanks for the chat, Abby,' she said, following her out into the corridor. 'You'll let me know if there are any further developments?'

'There won't be,' Abby replied, well aware of the significance of Jean's meaningful look.

'Oh, Abby,' Sean said as she turned to go. 'I was wondering if you could come to my office at twelve?'

'Why?' she said warily, all too vividly remembering what had happened the last time she'd gone there.

His eyes gleamed for an instant and then his face grew serious. 'Tom Burton's coming in for his echocardiogram today and as you've been liaising with his GP I thought you might like to be there.'

'I'll be there,' she replied, and strode off down the corridor before he could say another word.

It did not take Jean more than a few minutes to countersign the cheques Sean had for her but instead of leaving as he had expected she sat down and regarded him thoughtfully.

'Something bothering you?' he asked.

'What are you playing at, Sean? And don't give me that little-boy-innocent look,' she added as his eyebrows rose quizzically. 'You've got Abby so confused she doesn't know whether she's on her head or her heels.'

'Did she tell you that?' he asked, a slight frown appearing on his forehead.

'Of course she didn't but I'm not blind or deaf. She was all set to marry Robert Forrest before you came along and started ruffling the waters. Leave well alone, Sean.'

'But she doesn't love Robert and I very much doubt whether he loves her.'

'And what's that to you?' Jean asked, her brown eyes fixed on him unwaveringly. 'Just suppose for one moment that you're successful in this little game of yours. You split them up—what then?'

'They'll find people they're more suited to,' he smiled.

Jean groaned in exasperation. 'Sean Maguire, there are times when I wish you were twenty-five years younger and I could put you over my knee and beat some sense into you!'

'Don't let my age hold you back,' he grinned.

She shook her head. 'People aren't pawns you can manipulate at will, Sean. They are human beings with feelings and hopes and needs of their own. You say Robert's not right for Abby—does that mean you think you are?'

'I'm not the marrying kind.'

'And what's that supposed to mean?' she demanded.

'According to Abby, it means that I enjoy playing around too much to want to shoulder some responsibility,' he said wryly.

'Is she right?'

'Of course she isn't,' he protested, a slight tinge of colour appearing on his cheeks. 'All it means is I like my life the way it is. I can go where I want, do what I want and see who I want. Why would I want to change?'

'Why indeed?' Jean said drily and then sighed. 'Someone is going to get hurt, you know.'

'No one's going to get hurt. All I'm doing is showing Abby what any other person with half a brain would know already—that if she marries Robert Forrest it will be a total disaster.'

Jean gazed at him for a minute and then got to her feet. 'Do you know what I think you need?'

'A swift kick up the backside?' he said, his eyes dancing.

She chuckled. 'Apart from that! What you need, my friend, is to fall in love—really fall in love—and for the woman to put you through hell. That would knock some of the arrogance out of you.'

Sean threw back his head and laughed. 'Dream on, Jean, dream on!'

Her words, however, had struck home. For a long time after she'd gone he sat motionless at his desk, ignoring the tray full of unanswered correspondence awaiting his attention. Jean was right. He had no business interfering in Abby's life and he hadn't set out to, not at the beginning. At the beginning all he'd wanted was to inflict a sharp dent on her supreme confidence that only she knew what was best for Ardmar, and if ruffling her emotionally would inflict that dent then he'd been quite prepared to do it.

Now—now he wasn't at all sure of his motives. Abby could be all too likeable when she wasn't biting his head off but he had no intention of getting involved with a member of his staff, and certainly not with a freckle-faced, red-headed virago. Keeping Abby off balance was one thing, becoming emotionally involved with her was a whole different ball game—a game he had no intention of playing.

He laughed out loud suddenly. What the heck was he getting so worried about? He wasn't doing anything so dreadful. He was simply showing Abby that Robert wasn't the man for her—and he wasn't. She wouldn't fall in love with him and he sure as hell wasn't going to fall in love with her. One day he was sure Abby

would thank him for his interference—and on that
complacent thought he picked up his pen and attacked
his correspondence.

Far from showing any gratitude towards Sean, Abby
was at that very moment staring at Robert in barely
concealed fury.

'You've invited Sean out to dinner with us? Oh,
Robert, *why*? I see enough of him as it is at work
without having to socialise with him as well!'

Robert's jaw set. 'I thought it would be a nice
gesture—and I'm not cancelling,' he added as she
made to speak. 'I'd look a proper idiot if I did.'

Abby seethed inwardly. Robert didn't often dig in
his heels but one look at his implacable countenance
was enough to convince her that this was one of
those times.

'And when is this jolly event supposed to take
place?' she asked tightly.

'Saturday. I thought we'd take him to the Rogano—
and I've asked Carol to join us.'

'Carol?' she repeated.

'She's only been here five months,' he replied
defensively, 'and Sean needs a partner.'

Then why can't Carol go out with him and I'll stay
home? she was tempted to say but didn't.

'It will be fun,' Robert said bracingly. 'You'll
enjoy it.'

Enjoy it? Abby thought waspishly. Enjoy spending
an entire evening in Sean's company, having to endure
his barbed comments, his sly innuendos about Robert
and her? She'd rather spend a night having her eyelashes pulled out one by one!

'I'm on an early lunch-hour today—want to join
me?' Robert asked, clearly taking her silence for
acquiescence to his suggestion.

Abby shook her head. 'I've a meeting with Sean in ten minutes.'

'Cheer up,' Robert smiled, kissing her lightly. 'It may never happen.'

It already has, she thought angrily as she made her way to Sean's office. Somehow she had to cut this man down to size. The only problem was she didn't have the faintest idea of how to do it.

'Punctual as ever,' Sean smiled when she knocked on his office door.

'Punctual and polite,' she said, taking a seat. 'I remembered to knock,' she added as his eyebrows rose questioningly.

'Sorry about earlier,' he grinned. 'Now this shouldn't take long—'

'You are remembering the hospital bursar's due at quarter past twelve, Dr Maguire?' Molly Jordan asked as she handed him Tom Burton's case-notes.

'Quarter past twelve?' Abby repeated. 'But that means you're only giving the Burtons fifteen minutes of your time, Sean.'

'Which will be more than enough to explain the procedure,' he replied.

Conscious that Molly Jordan's sharp green eyes were fixed on her, Abby said nothing. He was, as he had reminded her so often, the boss.

'Before the Burtons arrive,' Sean continued as Molly closed the door behind her, 'I'd just like to say something about what happened when we got back from Cawdor—'

'I think the less we say about that the better,' she cut in, all smooth efficiency and calmness on the outside though inside her stomach had flipped over uncomfortably.

'OK,' he said with clear reluctance, 'but I just want

you to know I don't make a habit of kissing members
of my medical team.'

'I think Alastair Bell and Joe Ferguson will be might-
ily relieved to hear that,' she said lightly.

He threw back his head and laughed and Abby's
heart contracted painfully. Why did he have to be so
attractive? Why, out of all the hospitals he could have
chosen, did Sean have to choose Ardmar? She had
been happy with her life, settled in it, and now increasingly all she felt was confused and bewildered.

'I'm sorry if we're a bit late,' Gilly Burton apolo-
gised, her face white and drawn with apprehension, as
Molly ushered her and her husband into the office.
'The motorway was much busier than we expected.'

'That road can be hell at this time of year, can't it?'
Abby smiled sympathetically as she pulled two seats
forward for the couple. 'It took me two hours to drive
thirty miles last summer—one of the prices we pay for
living in an area that draws tourists like a magnet, I'm
afraid.'

'We got stuck behind a whole line of caravans,'
Roger Burton sighed. 'Sunday drivers, most of them,
and Gilly didn't want me to overtake—not with Tom
in the back.'

The conversation consisted of trivialities but Abby
sensed the Burtons' anxiety, their initial need to talk
about anything other than what was going to happen
to their son. Sean was shuffling his papers, clearly
anxious to get on with the proceedings, but she ignored
him. If he'd been stupid enough to schedule another
appointment too close to this one it was his own
damn fault.

'Can I hold Tom?' she asked, holding out her arms
to take the sleeping two-year-old from his mother. 'Oh,
he's beautiful. He's like you, Gilly, though I have to
say I think he has Roger's nose.'

'Dr Hunter—if we could progress with the matter in hand?' Sean said, his voice barely disguising his irritation.

'Go right ahead, Dr Maguire,' she said sweetly.

Sean shot her a sideways glance that said all too clearly, Don't get smart with me, and then turned to the Burtons. 'As you both know, Tom is scheduled for an echocardiogram this morning. It's a non-invasive diagnostic procedure—'

'Invasive?' Roger Burton interrupted, staring at Sean in open dismay. 'You mean you're going to operate? I thought Tom was simply having some tests done.'

'He is,' Abby said reassuringly. 'A non-invasive procedure is just a doctor's way of saying a test.'

'Thank you for clarifying that for us, Dr Hunter,' Sean declared, his eyebrows snapping down. 'As I was about to say,' he added, with the unspoken words 'until I was so rudely interrupted' left hanging in the air, 'the echocardiography will reveal whether Tom has a congenital heart defect or not.'

'Congenital?' Roger echoed blankly.

'A defect Tom might have been born with,' Abby explained. 'Some children are born with defects—we call them congenital. Other children develop heart conditions as they grow older.'

'Thank you once more, Dr Hunter,' Sean said tightly, and then proceeded to explain at length exactly how an echocardiography examination worked.

Abby sighed as she watched the Burtons' bewildered faces. They didn't understand a word he was saying and the more they didn't understand, the more frightened they were becoming. Sean was going to hate her for it but she just couldn't sit silently by watching their growing anxiety.

'An echocardiogram is really just a rather long-winded name we give to a machine that uses ultrasound waves to examine the heart from the outside,' she said, cutting across Sean's description deliberately. 'Have you seen those old war movies where there's a ship on the surface of the sea and they think there's a submarine under the water—?'

'And you hear bleep-bleep noises when they locate it?' Gilly said with dawning comprehension.

Abby nodded. 'It's a bit like that. The echoes are recorded on a screen so we get a very clear picture of what's going on in Tom's heart.'

'But how can Tom have heart disease?' Gilly continued, gazing down at her son. 'Look at him—he seems perfectly healthy—and no one said anything when he was born, did they, Roger?' she added, turning to her husband for confirmation. 'Could our GP have made a mistake, Dr Maguire?'

'It isn't always possible to diagnose heart disease at birth, Mrs Burton,' he replied. 'A child can sometimes manage quite happily for years with a defective heart before a problem is discovered. I think I've got that right, haven't I, Dr Hunter?' he added, his lip curling slightly. 'Or perhaps you'd care to correct me?'

Faint colour appeared on Abby's cheeks. The situation was getting ridiculous. They were like two dogs fighting over a bone and yet all she was trying to do was help.

'Is he going to die, Doctor?' Gilly murmured, her bottom lip trembling, her eyes fixed not on Sean, to Abby's acute embarrassment, but on her.

'There are lots of things we can do even if there is a problem,' Abby said encouragingly. 'Ninety per cent of cases like these are acyanotic—'

'That means the baby's blood isn't flowing properly, doesn't it, Dr Hunter?' Sean interrupted, the sarcasm in his voice all too clear.

'If Tom's blood isn't flowing properly it could be due to an obstruction like a narrowed valve,' she said smoothly, deliberately ignoring his jibe. 'There is the possibility, however, that there could be something wrong with the structure of the heart—a defect like a hole—'

'A hole in his heart?' Roger said, gripping his wife's hand tightly. 'If he has a hole in his heart won't he die?'

Abby glanced across at Sean.

'You want me to contribute something?' he said in mock amazement. 'How refreshing!'

She bit her lip and willed herself not to react. The last thing the Burtons wanted or needed was to witness a full-scale row between the two of them.

'We won't know anything for sure about Tom's condition until we get the results back, Mr Burton,' Sean said. 'Even if he does have a hole in his heart, some holes heal themselves without the need for surgery.'

'And the others?'

'Let's not cross bridges until we come to them,' Sean replied.

'And even if Tom does require surgery there's so much we can do nowadays,' Abby could not help but add. 'Medical science has progressed in leaps and bounds over the last ten years, so please try not to worry.'

The couple smiled weakly.

'Perhaps you'd both like to go through to Molly Jordan?' Sean said, getting to his feet. 'There are some papers you need to sign and I understand Staff Nurse Mackay is waiting to take you down to the ward—No, not you, Dr Hunter,' he added, his tone clipped, as she made to follow the couple. 'I'd like a word.'

It wasn't a request, it was a command, and her heart sank. She closed the door behind the Burtons and waited for the explosion to come.

'Don't you ever—*ever*—do that to me again!' he said, his voice like a whiplash.

'You asked me to sit in—'

'To sit in, not to take over the whole interview!' he retorted. 'You completely undermined my authority; you talked to the Burtons as though they were children—explaining every word I said—'

'And you talked to them as though they were fourth-year medical students,' she flared. 'They're parents, Sean—frightened, bewildered parents.'

'Are you presuming to give me lessons in diagnosis now?' he demanded, his lips setting into a tight line.

'Of course I'm not,' she protested. 'I'm just trying to make you see that your approach was all wrong—'

'*My approach was all wrong*?' he echoed, his expression so furious that she quailed inwardly. 'All that was wrong with my approach was that I had to compete with a Little Miss Echo twittering on in the background! My God, if I didn't know better I'd say you deliberately set out to make me look ridiculous.'

'Oh, I don't think you needed my help to do that—I'd say you managed it very nicely all by yourself!' she snapped back.

White-faced with anger, he took a step towards her and then stopped, realising that though part of him wanted to shake her until her teeth rattled the other part—the overwhelming part—wanted to pull her into his arms and kiss her until she begged him to stop.

Unconsciously he shook his head. He had always made it a rule never to get involved with his staff. It led to too many complications, to awkward matters of discipline, but he was bewilderingly aware of the attraction he felt towards this woman—an attraction that was both unfamiliar and inexplicable.

'You meant well, Sean, I know you did,' Abby was continuing, totally unaware of the thoughts that were going through his head, 'but you talked at the Burtons like a hospital doctor—'

'I am a hospital doctor,' he said grimly.

'You're not listening to me,' she declared. 'I said you talked *at* them. Haven't you heard the old medical joke—GPs go into general practice because they like people, hospital doctors stay in hospitals because they don't have to?'

'Just what are you trying to say?' he said slowly.

'I've seen you with the children—you're good with them. Well, adults are just bigger children—'

'That's the most patronising thing I've ever heard anyone say!' he broke in angrily.

'I'm not being patronising!' she cried. 'When people meet a doctor in a professional capacity all their confidence goes out the window and sometimes we don't help them. It's all too easy to let an invisible wall grow between us and the people we see—'

'You're saying I don't care?' he exclaimed, his eyes cold, hard—like stones.

'No, of course I'm not,' she said in exasperation. 'But you've come from a large hospital, a hospital where you saw dozens, maybe hundreds of people every day in the full knowledge that perhaps—if you were lucky—you could give each patient ten minutes of your time. The only way you could survive was to build a wall of medical jargon in front of you, a wall that said "I'm the doctor, I'm the expert; don't question me". At Ardmar we've all the time in the world; we don't need the wall.'

He stared at her, horribly aware that she might be right. When he'd started out in medicine he had been determined never to short-change a patient, never to hide behind the authority of his white coat, but as he'd climbed the promotion ladder the demands of his heavy schedule had gradually taken precedence over everything else.

Had he lost touch? Had he lost the ability to talk to patients? The thought appalled him and he lashed out at the only person he could.

'You're always so right, aren't you?' he said, his voice shaking with anger. 'You're always so bloody right. Wonderful Dr Hunter, perfect Dr Hunter—Dr Hunter who can't even run her own damn personal life without cocking it up!'

She whitened and instantly he regretted his words but she didn't give him the chance to apologise.

'That was a cheap shot—even from you,' she asserted, her eyes blazing. 'Let me tell you this. You may have qualifications a mile long and you may have experience coming out of your ears but when it comes to knowing how to deal with people you're as ignorant as a hermit!'

'Finished?' he said, his voice caustic.

'With you, yes,' she said, horribly aware that she was near to tears. 'Completely and utterly!'

She was still trembling with rage when she reached the hospital canteen. How could she have been so blind? she thought furiously as she forced the bitter coffee down her throat in an attempt to calm herself. She had told Jean only that morning how good Sean was at his job. Good at his job! He didn't deserve to be left in charge of a hamster, far less a hospital!

And yet you're still attracted to him, a little voice reminded her—a voice she tried to crush down. You're a fool, Abby Hunter, she thought bitterly. A complete and utter fool.

'Dr Hunter!'

Advancing purposefully towards her across the canteen was the rotund form of George Benson. This was all she needed today, she thought with a groan.

'I'm looking for Dr Maguire,' he declared, easing himself onto the seat opposite her, 'and he's not in his office.' He made it sound like a capital offence.

'He could be in one of the wards or the day-care centre,' she suggested.

'But he knew I was coming in today for one of my monthly visits.' George frowned.

Abby said nothing. She was done with defending Sean Maguire.

'The day-care centre, you said?' George repeated petulantly. 'Would you walk there with me, my dear? There are one or two things I'd like to discuss with you after I've seen Dr Maguire—the hospital laundry bill for one. It seems inordinately high to me.'

Abby gritted her teeth and got to her feet. The laundry bill—well, she guessed that was a slight promotion in George's eyes.

'How's Dr Maguire shaping up?' George continued as they went out of the main building and along to the annexe.

'It's early days,' she said tersely.

'Not committing yourself, eh? Sensible girl.' He smiled and then frowned slightly. 'What *is* that noise?'

Abby had heard it too. 'It sounds like some of the children, Mr Benson.'

'It sounds more like a riot,' he said, striding towards the door of the day centre and throwing it open.

As Abby peered over his shoulder she could scarcely believe her eyes. The noise of twenty children in full cry was incredible enough but it was the man in the middle of it all who caught her attention, the man wearing the lopsided headdress of feathers, the man brandishing the plastic tomahawk with gay abandon, the man she had decided shouldn't be left in charge of a hamster, far less a patient.

It was a Sean she didn't recognise, a Sean who didn't

give a damn if he looked ridiculous as long as the children were enjoying themselves—and they were; they were loving every minute of it. Even Charlie White, who had scarcely said a word since he'd started attending the day-care centre, was whooping and shrieking with the best of them.

'What is the meaning of this exhibition?' George Benson bellowed, his face almost puce with rage.

Instant silence reigned—a silence broken only by a couple of nervous giggles and a small sob.

Sean lowered the tomahawk slowly and pulled off his feathers, looking more uncomfortable and embarrassed than Abby would have believed possible. 'Come to see some occupational therapy, have you, Mr Benson?' he said with a small smile.

'I'd call it complete mayhem, Dr Maguire,' George Benson said icily. 'These children are ill—'

'Not so ill that a little fun will do them any harm,' Sean interrupted.

'A little *fun*?' George repeated, drawing himself up to his full five feet five. 'You call this *fun*? I confess I've never been more shocked in my life!'

'You don't get out a lot, then, Mr Benson?' Sean suggested, his eyes filled with laughter.

A giggle came from one of the children—a giggle that was quickly smothered as George whirled round to fix the offender with a withering stare.

'I don't know what is considered acceptable behaviour from a chief of staff down south, Dr Maguire,' George declared, turning back to him, 'but I can assure you we take a very dim view of such an exhibition at Ardmar. Suppose I'd had one of our benefactors with me instead of Dr Hunter?'

'Then he or she would have seen some happy children,' Sean replied.

'They would have seen the head of this hospital

behaving in a reprehensible way!' George retorted.
'You have not heard the end of this, Dr Maguire—
not by a long shot. When the board hear my and Dr
Hunter's testimonies about this. . .this debacle, you
could well be looking for new employment—is that
not so, Dr Hunter?'

Abby gazed at George Benson and then across at
Sean. He could not have hung himself more effectively
if he'd tried. One condemning word from her to the
board and he would be out of her hair and out of the
hospital for good.

'Is that not so, Dr Hunter?' Mr Benson repeated,
his small brown eyes fixed pointedly on her.

If she had met George immediately after the interview with the Burtons she doubted if she'd have
hesitated for a minute, and yet now. . . She cleared
her throat slightly, aware that Sean was watching her.

'I don't see that Dr Maguire has done anything
worthy of censure, Mr Benson,' she said quietly.

'*What*?' George Benson exploded.

'Look at the children,' she said. 'They're happy—
what more could we ask?'

George Benson's colour mounted quite alarmingly
and for a split second Abby wondered whether he
was going to have a seizure, but before she could say
anything he had turned on his heel and stormed out
of the door.

A cheer went up from the children but Abby didn't
wait to see Sean's reaction. She ran quickly out of the
annexe, hoping to placate George before he left the
premises, but she was too late; his car was already
racing down the drive. She shook her head and sighed.
He was going to make a bad enemy, of that she
was sure.

'Thanks.'

She turned to see that Sean had followed her.

'I thought my goose was well and truly cooked,' he continued, thrusting his hand through his already dishevelled black hair, 'and it would have been if you hadn't backed me up.'

'You sound surprised,' she said.

'Don't you think I have a right to be?' he asked. 'After this morning I'd have thought you'd be only too delighted to get rid of me. Why did you support me?'

She stared past him at the dark waters of the Moray Firth sparkling in the sunshine. Part of her knew that she'd done it because he'd shown her how much he cared for the children, but the other part—the part she hated—knew that there was another, purely personal reason.

'Let's just say George Benson isn't my favourite person,' she replied.

'And?'

'And what?' She frowned.

'Oh, come on, Abby, that's not the only reason,' he pressed, his eyes fixed on her intently.

'Ok,' she smiled, 'so I'm acknowledging you can be good at your job—satisfied?'

'More than satisfied!' he exclaimed, though she thought he looked strangely disappointed. 'An accolade like that from you demands a brass band, fanfares—'

'Sarcasm is the lowest form of wit, Sean Maguire,' she interrupted severely, though her eyes danced.

'I owe you—and more especially the Burtons—an apology, don't I?' he said ruefully.

'The Burtons are fine and I've got broad shoulders.'

A small chuckle broke from him.

'My broad shoulders are funny?' she protested.

He shook his head. 'I'm just wondering what dreadful crime I must have committed in a former life that made the gods decide to appoint you my nemesis.'

She grimaced slightly. 'Is that how you see me?'

'No,' he smiled, reaching up to brush a stray tendril of hair back from her face.

The touch of his hand against her skin was electrifying. Their eyes locked and an awkward silence fell, a silence she couldn't have broken to save herself.

'I suppose I'd better get back to those kids before they actually start scalping someone for real,' he said at last.

'I suppose you should,' she replied, conscious that her heart was beating very fast and her mouth was dry.

For a few seconds Sean gazed down at her and then he suddenly wheeled about and walked away.

She stared after him for a moment, feeling oddly bereft and alone, and then dug her shaking hands deep into the pockets of her white coat. Abby Hunter, she told herself firmly as she began to walk back to the main building, you need your head examined!

CHAPTER FIVE

IT WAS the shrill, insistent ringing of the phone that woke Abby. Reluctantly she stuck out her arm and dragged the receiver down under the bedclothes.

'Yes?' she muttered.

'Did I wake you?'

She recognised the voice immediately. 'It's two o'clock in the morning, Sean. What the hell did you think I was doing—limbo-dancing?'

A deep chuckle came down the phone. 'Sorry, but we've got a possible ruptured appendix here—can you assist?'

She was wide awake now. 'Who is it?'

'Christopher Paterson.'

She was already pulling off her nightdress. 'Give me ten minutes and I'll be there.'

She made it in eight, to find Sean already scrubbed up and ready to go.

'What happened?' she said. 'He seemed OK when we took him to Cawdor.'

He shrugged. 'You know as well as I do that appendixes can act up out of the blue.'

'You're sure it's his appendix?' she asked, and then bit her lip as his eyebrows rose. 'Sorry—stupid question.'

'I'm sure.' He smiled without rancour. 'He has got all the classic symptoms—stomach pain, sickness, rigid and distended abdomen.'

'Any sign of peritonitis?' she asked anxiously.

'We won't know anything for sure until we get in there so could you scrub up as quickly as possible?'

She nodded and went to change. It had been a long time since she'd assisted in such a procedure. Mentally she reviewed the operation in her mind as she scrubbed up, praying that she wouldn't forget anything. It was a tricky enough operation on a child without a disability but on a child with cerebral palsy so much could go wrong. She took a deep breath as she tied on her mask. She had told Sean she could assist; she couldn't back out now.

Within minutes she was back in the operating theatre. Alastair Bell looked white-faced and nervous behind his mask as he sat by the anaesthetics trolley and Sister Mackay looked equally tense. In fact the only person who appeared totally unconcerned was the man who was actually going to carry out the operation, Abby thought ruefully.

'Is he out yet, Alastair?' Sean asked, the surgical knife poised in his hand.

'Fast asleep, Sean,' Alastair replied.

'How's his pressure?'

'Good.'

'OK, everyone,' Sean said in a voice that suggested that operating at twenty past two in the morning on a child with cerebral palsy was the most normal thing in the world, 'let's go to work.'

As Sean made his incision into Christopher's stomach Abby felt as though someone was cutting into her. They were operating on the child whose only aspiration was to return to Cawdor to see his beloved ducks; they were trying to save the life of the child who had said he was friendless because he was disabled.

Quickly she sent up a silent prayer. Please don't let anything happen to this child, she prayed. Please let what we're doing work. And then there was no time to think of anything but the role she had to play as she handed Sean a succession of instruments.

'There's the little blighter,' he observed at last, 'and it has ruptured, damn it.'

He was right; the appendix was no longer intact and an abscess was clearly visible.

'Right, we'll remove the appendix first—could you stand by with the drain, Abby?'

She nodded. The abscess could not be surgically removed. A drain had to be placed in the stomach during the operation and then the fluids from the abscess would be drained into an external bag over a period of hours.

With a speed and skill Abby could only admire Sean removed the appendix.

'How's his pressure, Alastair?' he asked, glancing over at him.

'Holding.'

Quickly Abby inserted the drain into the abscess cavity and then attached it to the drainage bag.

'OK, let's close,' Sean said. 'Well done, everyone,' he added. 'We're not out of the woods yet but we're beginning to see daylight.'

A collective sigh of relief went up from everyone. Sean was right—they weren't home and dry yet. The infection caused by the ruptured appendix could spread and generalised peritonitis might develop, but if it didn't Christopher should make a complete recovery.

'I want a careful watch kept on him for the next few days, Sister Mackay,' Sean said as he pulled off his surgical gloves. 'Any abdominal pain, vomiting, or signs that his abdomen is becoming rigid again—phone me at once. The last thing we want is him going into shock.'

'Christopher's parents are outside, Dr Maguire,' she told him. 'I think they'd appreciate a word.'

'OK, Sister. Will you wait for me, Abby?' he added quickly as she pulled down her mask.

Now that the operation was over her tired brain screamed a protest. She could really do without an in-depth discussion of the procedure. All she wanted was her bed.

'Please?' he pressed, seeing her reluctance.

In the harsh theatre lights he looked exhausted, almost vulnerable, and she found herself nodding.

By the time Sean had comforted and reassured Christopher's worried parents and checked on Christopher in Recovery Abby was almost asleep in one of the large leather armchairs in the hospital entrance hall.

'Sorry,' he said as she rubbed her eyes wearily. 'It took a bit longer than I thought.'

'It's OK,' she replied, uncurling her legs and standing up. 'You look rough,' she added, taking in his unshaven chin and the fatigue in his eyes.

'You look—' He paused. 'Different.'

'I didn't know this was supposed to be a fashion show,' she protested, well aware that the old baggy sweater and jeans she'd thrown on in her rush to the hospital did nothing for her.

'I didn't mean different dreadful,' he said slowly. 'I meant different good.'

She stared at him for a second and then shook her head. 'Quarter to four in the morning and you can still switch on the charm—you're some operator, Sean Maguire!'

A slight frown appeared on his forehead. 'Is that what you think I'm doing—switching on the charm, as you phrase it?'

'I don't *think*—I *know* it,' she laughed. 'Now, why did you ask me to wait?'

'I wanted some company—simple as that,' he said. 'After an operation I find it almost impossible to relax.

How about sharing some breakfast with me at my place?'

'Breakfast?' she repeated, feeling her stomach heave at the thought. 'At this time in the morning?'

'It hardly seems worth while going back to bed when we're only going to have to get up again in a couple of hours.'

'Speak for yourself,' she retorted. 'My bed seems very inviting at the moment.'

His eyes gleamed. 'I can't argue with that—I'd say your bed sounds very inviting at the moment.'

She gazed at him severely. 'Breakfast, you said?'

'Breakfast,' he sighed in mock defeat, leading the way outside, only to stop short on the hospital steps. 'It's light,' he said in amazement.

'Of course it is,' she replied. 'We're so far north here, it rarely gets dark at all in the summer months.'

'But how do the birds manage—know when to start the dawn chorus?'

'Are you serious?' she exclaimed, opening her car door. 'Look, at this time in the morning I can just about get my brain round saying good morning. If it's a debate on ornithological matters you want, you've got the wrong girl!'

He grinned broadly. 'Sorry—see you at my place in ten minutes.'

It was only when she reached his cottage that she wondered at the wisdom of her decision. Every time she'd been alone with him—and each of those times they had been in a purely professional capacity—he had managed to throw her totally off balance and yet here she was voluntarily putting herself in the same position again.

For a second she debated driving away and then shook her head. She was thirty years old, for heaven's sake, not some adolescent schoolgirl out on her first date. She could handle this man, she told herself firmly as she got out of her car and made her way into his cottage.

'I've cornflakes, fruit juice, toast, coffee, and I can scramble some eggs if you want,' he said when she joined him in the kitchen.

'Sounds great.'

'I meant what do you want?' he asked.

'The lot,' she replied, suddenly discovering that she was actually rather hungry.

His eyebrows rose slightly but he said nothing.

'Do you think Christopher will be OK?' she asked, helping herself to some fruit juice.

'Should be—we just have to watch out for him going into shock.'

She nodded. 'I've often wondered what it must be like to be the parent of someone like Christopher. We're supposed to be trained to deal with the situation and yet we find it hard. What must it be like if the child is yours, or related to you in some way, and to know each day you have with them is a bonus?'

'It's absolute hell.'

Her eyes flew to his face and then away again quickly on seeing the raw pain there. What did he mean? Did he mean he had a disabled child or that someone in his family had? He had told her he'd never married— had he lied or was he divorced or widowed? Questions raced through her brain, questions she knew she had no right to ask, and deliberately she poured herself out some cornflakes and sat down at the table.

'You're a remarkable woman, Abby Hunter,' he observed as he joined her. 'No questions, no inquisition?'

'It's not for me to pry,' she said simply.

A small smile curved his lips. 'You mean that, don't you?'

'I wouldn't have said it otherwise,' she said in surprise.

'No, I don't think you would,' he said, gazing at her thoughtfully. 'My sister Sinead's boy had leukaemia.'

'Had—you mean—'

'He died when he was ten.'

'I'm so sorry,' she murmured, knowing how inadequate the words sounded but unable to think of anything else to say.

'All the training I had, all the skill, and yet when it came right down to it I was about as much use to my sister as the average man in the street,' he said bleakly. 'For four years we went through treatment after treatment, hoping, praying, and for four years I knew Sinead was watching me, willing me to cure Conor, and I couldn't. . .I couldn't.

'When he died I threw myself into my work, trying to forget, but nothing helped. That's why I came to Ardmar. I had this crazy idea, you see, that maybe my skills might make a difference here once in a while, that I'd be able to lay the ghost of my sister's face when I had to tell her there was nothing I could do.'

So he *had* possessed an ulterior motive for applying for the chief of staff's job. She had been right but she took no pleasure in the thought.

'These cornflakes are nice,' she said awkwardly.

'Good,' he smiled, some of the pain in his eyes easing. 'Are you sure you want scrambled eggs as well?' he continued, reaching over to light the stove.

'Good grief, do you mean Molly Jordan hasn't told you I'm the original dustbin where food is concerned?' she queried. 'According to hospital gossip—which in this case is accurate, I'm afraid—if you stand on my foot my mouth opens automatically.'

A burst of laughter came from him. 'Well, all I can say is you're looking good on it,' he said, his eyes running appreciatively over her figure.

'Baggy sweaters hide a multitude of sins.' She sighed ruefully. 'So do white coats, thank God.'

'Women should have curves where they're supposed to have curves,' he observed. 'I wouldn't want to take a bag of bones to bed.'

A flush of colour crept up her neck. 'That comment conjures up a very weird image of your sleeping habits, I'm afraid,' she said, and he laughed again.

'You're good company, Abby Hunter.'

'I'm well-known for it!' she exclaimed. 'Good old Abby, good listener, good friend, that's me.'

The laughter in his eyes died. 'Why do you always do that—put yourself down? I tell you you're good company and you make it sound like a fault. If I try to compliment you about your looks you treat it as a joke. Why can't you ever accept a compliment as though it was genuinely meant?'

'Force of habit, I guess. All my life I've known I was plain—no, it's true,' she said as he tried to interrupt. 'I used to hear my aunt and uncle telling their friends how lucky it was that Abby had brains because she'd never get by on her looks. I came to terms with it a long time ago. You don't have to pay me meaningless compliments.'

'But you're not plain, Abby,' he protested, reaching across and tilting her chin. 'You have lovely eyes and that hair of yours is so beautiful—'

'Don't!' she cried quickly, her brown eyes suddenly showing such pain that he gazed at her in total bewilderment. 'Don't say another word, not. . .not another word!'

'But Abby—'

'No, not another word—I mean it, Sean,' she said, closing her eyes tightly, knowing that the last thing she wanted to hear from him was the kind of lies that had tripped so easily from Michael's lips. She could handle just about anything, but she couldn't handle that.

He got to his feet and busied himself with the eggs for a minute, but when he turned back his face was determined. 'You've two choices, Abby. You can go out to your car and drive away or you can tell me what I've said that's so upset you—but I warn you, if you drive away I won't let the subject drop—I'll bring it up again and again until you give me an answer.'

She stared bleakly down into her empty bowl, knowing that he meant what he'd said. 'I just can't bear lies and pretence, that's all,' she said at last.

'Why would you think I'd lie about the way you look?' he asked in confusion.

She said nothing.

'All right,' he continued, 'what do you think I see when I look at you?'

'An interfering, bloody-minded nuisance?' she suggested.

He grinned. 'Apart from that, what do you think I see?'

She sighed. 'A girl with red hair and freckles—a girl with brown eyes and freckles—oh, I don't know, Sean. Does it matter?'

'To me it does,' he replied. 'I'll tell you what I see, shall I? I see a woman I like very much. I see a pair of big brown eyes and incredible eyelashes. I see hair that's as fiery as an autumn leaf, hair I've been longing to run my fingers through for ages. That's what I see.'

Her eyes showed her disbelief and something else— something very like cynicism—and he frowned. 'Who was he, Abby?'

She shifted uneasily in her seat but she was too tired, too drained, to prevaricate. 'His name was Michael.'

'And he hurt you?' he said gently.

She nodded as unwanted shafts of memory rose inside her.

'Tell me about him,' he said, clearing her empty bowl away and placing a steaming plate of scrambled eggs in front of her.

'It's a long story.'

'I'm going nowhere,' he replied.

She didn't want to tell him but she knew he wouldn't let it rest until she did. 'I met Michael in my first year at med school. He was in his fourth year and there wasn't a girl in the school who wouldn't have given her right arm to date him.'

'He was that good-looking, huh?'

'Oh, yes,' she murmured, her lips curving slightly into a bitter smile. 'Michael was so handsome—and he was bright too.'

'I'm beginning to dislike him already,' he smiled, but Abby, he noticed, didn't.

'I couldn't believe it when he asked me out—a man like Michael wanting to date me—plain, ordinary me—and it wasn't just the once. He kept on asking me out and when he said he loved me it was like. . .oh, it was like having all your birthdays and Christmases in one.'

'What happened?' Sean asked, filling her cup with coffee and pouring out some for himself.

She pushed her plate of eggs away untouched, her appetite gone. 'Alarm bells should have gone off in my head when he started breaking dates but his excuses were so good, you see.'

She paused and then shook her head as the memories resurfaced. 'Actually his excuses were pretty pitiful but it's amazing how gullible a woman can be when she's in love. I discovered what was going on eventually. I went round to his flat one night to cook him a surprise meal and found him in bed with one of my girlfriends.'

She got to her feet quickly, unable to bear the sympathy in Sean's eyes, and moved over to one of the large armchairs by the unlit fire, cradling her coffee in her hands. 'I should just have accepted it, chalked it up to experience, but I didn't. I did the stupidest thing in the world. I confronted him in the university canteen and do you know what he did, Sean? He laughed. In front of all those people he laughed at me.'

'Oh, Abby—'

She waved away his outstretched hand, blinking the tears back from her eyes. 'You could have heard a pin drop in that canteen when he asked me how in the world I could ever have thought someone like him could love someone as plain as me. It had all been a joke, you see—nothing but a joke. He'd thought it would be amusing to take out the plainest girl at the university and make her think she was special.'

'He was a bastard,' Sean said, his voice tight.

'A truthful bastard at least.' She laughed shakily. 'Oh, Sean, you can have no idea what it feels like to be told you're worth nothing, less than nothing, by someone you love so much it hurts.'

He took the cup from her trembling hands and drew her into his arms. She didn't protest; she didn't resist. She simply rested her head on his shoulder with a sigh, taking comfort from the feel of two strong arms around her.

'The past is gone, Abby,' he murmured gently into her hair. 'Don't live in it, don't remember it, don't let it keep on hurting you.'

She shook her head and he lifted her chin, intending only to repeat his advice, but as he gazed at the tears shimmering on her eyelashes, the faint dusting of freckles that stood out in sharp relief to the whiteness of her skin he realised with a sudden shock that his body was stirring and hardening with desire. This wasn't supposed to happen. He wasn't supposed to feel like this. Let her go, his mind warned; just one kiss, his body urged, and his body won.

'No,' she whispered as his mouth sought hers.

'Hush,' he murmured, knowing already that one kiss was not enough, that the brief brushing of his lips against hers had not satisfied his desire but fuelled it.

He traced the soft contours of her face with his mouth, savouring the fluttering pulse at her throat, before returning to her lips again, thrusting his hands through her hair to lock her head closer to his. She gasped as he deepened the kiss, as his probing tongue awakened sensations she hadn't even known it was possible to experience, and she found herself returning his kiss, revelling in the groan he gave as she slid her fingers up his back to pull him closer, closer.

Somehow he had found the catch under her bulky sweater and released her bra and an overwhelming rush of longing coursed through her as his fingers curled around her erect nipples. Her own wetness told her how much she wanted him, that her body was demanding a closeness their clothes were impeding, and it would have been so easy to let go, to let herself be carried along on the strength of his touch, to forget everything. . .

But she couldn't. She couldn't forget the past, the resolution she'd made all those years ago that never again would her heart rule her head, and she pulled out of his arms and got to her feet, her breathing uneven and ragged.

'Abby—'

'This is a big mistake, Sean,' she murmured, her eyes bleak, her face vulnerable.

'How can it be a mistake?' he said. 'I know you want me as much as I want you.'

'Maybe right now I do—but right now I'm not thinking very straight,' she said shakily.

'Then don't think, just trust your feelings,' he told her, trying to draw her back into his arms without success.

'I don't do one-night stands, Sean—not for you, not for anyone.'

'It wouldn't be that,' he protested.

A half-smile appeared on her lips. 'No? How long would it be, then, before you moved on to someone else—two months—three? I can't handle that sort of uncertainty and I won't.'

'So there has to be an engagement ring on your finger—is that what you're saying?' he said, his voice harsh, as he grasped her hand and held it up to the light so that the sapphire and diamond cluster sparkled and gleamed.

She shook her head. 'I need commitment—long-term commitment. I need to feel secure, to know you'll be there if I need you—and that's not your style, Sean; you know it's not.'

He sat down on the arm of the seat, his eyes fixed on her. 'So that's it, is it? Just because you got badly burned in the past you're going to marry safe, dull Robert?'

'Robert is not dull,' she retorted, stung.

'But he's safe.'

'Is that so very bad?' she said, her voice breaking. 'Is it so very dreadful to decide to marry someone because they make you feel safe, secure?'

His eyes were suddenly compassionate, his smile unbelievably tender. 'No, of course it's not—not if you'd added another word—and it's a word I've never once heard you say, Abby. You've never once said you love him.'

'I do love him!' she protested, only to see him shake his head. 'All right, then, maybe I don't,' she added uncertainly, 'not in the wild romantic sense of love, but Robert's a good man, a kind man, and he loves me; he won't hurt me.'

He opened his mouth and then closed it again tightly and she reached for her car keys.

'I have to go, Sean. I want to shower before work.'

'Have your shower here.'

'Not advisable, I think.'

'You'd be quite safe, I can assure you,' he said mildly. 'It's only superheroes in films who can break down locked bathroom doors.'

A small smile was drawn from her. 'Thanks for the offer but I need a change of clothes anyway. No hard feelings, Sean?' she added as he walked with her to her car.

'None,' he declared, but when she got into her car he stayed her hand as she tried to shut the door. 'Abby, if you ever need someone to talk to—or a shoulder to cry on—promise you'll come to me?'

There was such urgency and intensity on his face that she frowned slightly. 'I can't see me ever needing to but if it makes you happy I'll promise. And, Sean,' she added, 'what happened between us—we just forget it, OK?'

'But Abby—'

'It's best, Sean,' she said firmly. 'We've both been a little fragile tonight and we've done things and said things we're going to bitterly regret later, so let's just forget it ever happened and go on as before.'

He nodded and she drove away quickly, knowing that if he had but touched her again her resolve would have broken, her barriers would all have come tumbling down.

Her rounds seemed endless that morning. She was tired, so tired, and it had nothing to do with her lack of sleep. Unbidden and unwanted, a face kept forcing itself into her consciousness, a face dominated by a pair of laughing grey eyes and a caressing smile.

He didn't love her; she knew he didn't. He wanted her, but he didn't love her. Perhaps another woman would have been satisfied with a relationship built on nothing but physical attraction but it wasn't enough for her. When the relationship ended, and end it surely would, she'd be devastated. She might be attracted to him but she couldn't go down that road to nowhere.

'You're looking tired, Abby,' Dr Ferguson commented when she popped her head round the door of Intensive Care to see how Christopher was.

'Interrupted sleep doesn't suit me, Joe,' she replied ruefully. 'How's Christopher?'

'Doing well.'

'Buzz me if there's the slightest change in his temperature, or if you feel at all uneasy about him,' she said as she stared down at Christopher's flushed face.

Joe nodded and Abby gently touched Christopher's cheek. He'd been so happy just a week ago when they'd gone to Cawdor, so concerned about the duck that didn't walk properly. 'Get well, Christopher,' she murmured. 'Get well and Dr Sean and I will take you back to Cawdor as many times as you want.'

'You should go home and get some sleep,' Joe Ferguson told her, noting the pallor of her skin, the dark shadows under her eyes.

'I'm going—I just want to call in on Becky Reid first.'

Joe twisted his stethoscope, his plump face uncomfortable. 'Sean isn't at all happy about her still being here, Abby. Carol Lennox says he virtually grinds his teeth every time he passes Becky's door.'

'I know,' she sighed. 'Have you heard how she is today?'

'As well as she's ever going to be,' Joe replied in a

tone that suggested that he, for one, agreed with Sean about Becky taking up a vitally needed bed.

Abby bit back the angry retort that sprang to her lips as she made her way up the stairs to the small side ward. No matter how she felt she desperately needed to keep as many of the medical staff on her side. Sean had made it clear that he wouldn't tolerate the situation for much longer and the more people she could get to support her the better.

Becky's head swivelled round keenly as it always did whenever anyone entered her room.

'How's my favourite patient this morning?' Abby said brightly, watching the light die in the child's eyes as she recognised her.

'I want. . .' Becky's voice trailed away and a frown appeared on her forehead.

'What? What do you want, Becky?' Abby asked.

'Daddy,' the child whispered. 'I want my daddy.'

Abby crushed down the hard lump in her throat. 'You'll see him soon, sweetheart; he'll come in soon— I promise.' But Becky simply turned her face to the wall with a sigh.

Sean was right, Abby thought as she walked slowly down the corridor. The situation couldn't go on like this, but how was she going to persuade Ben to see that though Becky could never be the child she was she could still give him great love and happiness?

She was still deep in thought when she rounded the corridor and walked straight into Robert and Carol.

'Good heavens, the pair of you look like a couple of conspirators!' she exclaimed, seeing Robert's flush of colour and Carol's clear embarrassment. 'If you're hatching some dastardly plot involving our esteemed chief of staff count me in!'

Robert laughed but Carol looked even more uncomfortable than ever.

'All ready for this dinner date of ours next Saturday, Carol?' Abby asked, wondering what on earth the girl had to look so embarrassed about.

'Looking forward to it,' Carol murmured.

'I can't say I am—no reflection on you, of course, Carol—but dinner out with my boss is not my idea of a fun evening,' Abby replied. 'It's all Robert's fault,' she added with mock severity. 'Once he gets a bee in his bonnet about something it's almost impossible to shift him.'

'I'd better go,' Carol said quickly. 'I'm due on duty in five minutes. Thanks for listening, Robert,' she added, her large blue eyes shimmering with what almost looked like unshed tears. 'It helped a lot.'

'Was it something I said?' Abby asked as she watched Carol's fast disappearing form.

'It's nothing to do with you,' Robert sighed. 'Her mother's just been diagnosed as having an inoperable cancer.'

'Oh, I'm sorry,' Abby said with concern. 'Should I go after her?'

He shook his head. 'She needs some space right now and I'm afraid this is the worst possible working environment for her—what with so many of our kids being on borrowed time.'

'But didn't she come to us from the A and E department?' Abby asked. 'That must have been pretty harrowing.'

'Yes, but sick kids always hit people the hardest,' Robert replied. 'It requires a very special kind of person to deal with it day in and day out and not everyone is as strong as you are, Abby.'

He didn't make it sound like a compliment and she stiffened. 'I care, Robert—God, how I care at times.'

'I know you do,' he said, catching her hand in his quickly. 'I didn't mean you don't care about your patients, I just meant. . .' His voice died away.

'What? What did you mean?' she demanded, and when he said nothing she shook her head with an irritation born of fatigue. 'Oh, Robert, sometimes I swear I don't understand you.'

'Only sometimes?' he said, his expression sad.

A distinct feeling of unease crept over her heart. 'What is it, Robert? What's wrong? You can talk to me—you know you can.'

He smiled with an effort. 'It's nothing—I'm just tired, I guess. I've got to go—I'll speak to you later.'

He walked away and it was only when he'd gone that she realised he hadn't kissed her. Always when they parted he kissed her, even if it was only a brief peck on her cheek. Something was bothering him; that much was obvious. Robert was usually so easygoing and yet today he seemed as taut as a wire.

And it wasn't just today, she realised. For the last month he'd been on edge, ill at ease in her company. She shook her head. She'd been neglecting him; that was the trouble. Since Sean had arrived her whole world had been turned upside down and unconsciously she had pushed Robert to the margin of her life. She would have to make it up to him, be especially nice to him at dinner on Saturday.

A sudden movement behind her caught her eye and she turned to find Sean in the corridor. From the look on his face he had clearly heard her conversation with Robert. Hot colour crept up her neck and she took a step towards him, only to stop as he turned and strode away from her quickly—but not quickly enough. There had been an expression on his face she didn't understand, an expression that almost looked like pity.

CHAPTER SIX

ABBY gazed down at the letter George Benson had given her to read and then up at him in disbelief. 'Is this some kind of a joke?'

'No joke, Dr Hunter,' he replied smoothly. 'Just a serious attempt to achieve something that would benefit us both.'

She stared down at the letter again, fighting to control her mounting anger. It was a letter to the board of governors, a letter of complaint about Sean, a letter purporting to come from her. All she needed to do was put her signature above where George had thoughtfully typed her name.

'You can't honestly think I'd sign that?' she said, barely able to keep the disgust from her voice.

'Not even for the chief of staff's job?' George asked with a smile she did not care for. 'And that's what we're talking about here, my dear.'

For two pins she would have liked to crumple the piece of paper into a tight ball and then stuff it down the throat of the man who sat so complacently opposite her, but she didn't. Instead she put the letter down on the desk between them and gazed at him thoughtfully.

'Why, Mr Benson? Why would you want to replace a man you told me only a few weeks ago was the answer to Ardmar's prayers?'

'No one—*no one*—makes me look a fool,' he answered, 'and certainly not a man I hired.'

'I thought the board appointed Dr Maguire, Mr Benson?' she said evenly.

His cheeks reddened. 'It amounts to the same thing.'

'I've no doubt the rest of the board would be very interested to hear that,' she said drily. 'So let me get this straight. You're suggesting that once Dr Maguire is sacked I'll be Ardmar's new chief of staff?'

'There is every possibility of that happening, yes,' he replied.

Like hell there was, she thought. She might be a fool to be attracted to a man like Sean but she wasn't so big a fool as to allow George to use her as a pawn in his own private war.

'How many copies of this have you got?' she said.

'None—I didn't think we'd want to risk it getting into the wrong hands.'

His cosy, confidential tone made her feel physically sick.

'I can see you're tempted, Dr Hunter,' he continued, clearly taking her silence for consideration of his idea.

She kept her temper—just. 'I'm not tempted in the least, Mr Benson. I think your actions are shoddy, underhanded and despicable—and I wonder how the rest of the board will feel when they see this,' she added, motioning to the letter. 'I think they'd be very interested, don't you?'

A smile appeared on his lips. 'It's not my name typed at the bottom of that letter, Dr Hunter, it's yours. And I don't see any witnesses to prove this conversation ever took place, do you?'

'What an odious little toad you are,' she said calmly, though inwardly she was seething. 'Get someone else to do your dirty work, Mr Benson—this lady's not for sale!'

She reached for the letter, intent on tearing it to shreds, but he got there first. 'I'll let your insults pass,' he murmured, though his eyes were hard. 'But I wouldn't be too hasty about this,' he continued as he got to his feet. 'Think about it, Dr Hunter; think about the opportunity you're letting slip by for want of a signature.

'I'll put it in here, shall I?' he said, opening her emergency medical bag and placing the letter in it. 'You might like to reconsider your position once you've had time to think.'

Perhaps a few weeks ago she might have wanted to think about it, but not now. Now she knew that no matter how personally unsettling she might find Sean he was the right man for the job.

'If that's all you came to see me about, Mr Benson, then I'll bid you good day.'

A flash of livid anger appeared for an instant on his face and then was gone. 'Just remember one thing, Dr Hunter,' he said as he paused on the threshold of her office. 'You might need a friend on the board one day and I can be a good friend—to people who help me.'

She couldn't stay in her office after he'd gone. The whole room felt polluted, tainted by his presence, and she made her way down the stairs intent on calling in on Christopher Paterson in Intensive Care, only to walk straight into Finlay Norris and Sean.

'Finlay, how nice to see you,' she said, forcing a smile to her lips for she was still furious. 'Is this a social call or business?'

'A bit of both,' he replied. 'Dr Maguire has been holding me hostage all morning in an attempt to squeeze more money out of me!'

'Successfully, I hope?' she chuckled.

'Oh, he's a smooth operator, this one, when he learns the ropes,' Finlay observed, his sharp blue eyes twinkling. 'He's managed to persuade me to contact all my business friends in London with a view to setting up a trust fund for Ardmar—but you probably know that already?'

She shook her head. 'Administration is Dr Maguire's pigeon, not mine.'

'But I thought the two of you worked as a team?' Finlay said in surprise.

'Dr Hunter has been as elusive as the scarlet pimpernel just lately,' Sean declared before she could say anything.

Abby's smile didn't slip for an instant though she knew that what Sean had said was true. For the last few days the merest glimpse of Sean's dark head at the end of a corridor or in the doorway to a ward had been enough to send her dashing to another part of the hospital to avoid him.

It wasn't that she was embarrassed to meet him again after that night in his cottage—well, OK, maybe she was, just a little—but what she most wanted was to be totally in control when she next talked to him.

'I've been busy,' she protested lightly. 'You know how it is—some weeks are busier than others.'

'Then you won't have heard of the fête Dr Maguire's thinking of holding in September?' Finlay continued. 'We're hoping to get Lesley Martin to open it.'

'The film star?' she exclaimed. 'I'm impressed.'

'As I said, this chief of staff of yours is some smooth operator—which is why I'm going now while I've still got a shirt on my back,' Finlay chuckled.

'He's that good?' Abby laughed.

'Take my tip—don't ever be alone with him,' he replied, mock serious. 'You wouldn't believe how persuasive he can be when he puts his mind to it!'

Oh, she would believe it, she thought as she watched Finlay walking away; she would most certainly believe it.

'You seem to be hitting it off well now with Finlay,' she observed as Sean accompanied her along the corridor.

'Who wouldn't after they'd had a few lessons at the Abby Hunter School of Communications?' he grinned.

'Do you think the trust fund will come off?' she asked as they made their way towards the stairs.

'With Finlay on our side it's got a better than average chance and it would certainly solve some of our immediate financial problems.'

'Damn—does that mean the striptease dancers are off?' she said, her eyes dancing.

'The what?' he asked, puzzled, and then dawning comprehension came into his face and he laughed. 'That was my suggestion the first time we met, wasn't it?'

'And I gave you quite an earful as I recall,' she chuckled.

'We've come a long way since then, haven't we?'

She looked up into his eyes. He looked tired and the urge to reach up and smooth away the lines of fatigue was almost irresistible. Deliberately she quickened her pace.

'George Benson is on the prowl,' she said. 'I've already had a visitation.'

'What did he want?'

'Your head on a block, basically. You've made a bad enemy there, Sean.'

'I can handle him,' he replied dismissively.

'I'd be careful if I were you,' she insisted. 'I know he seems like nothing more than a jumped-up little worm but he does exert considerable influence on the rest of the board.'

'As I said, I can handle him,' he declared. 'But thanks—for caring.'

There was a warmth in his voice that seemed to reach out and touch her, sending tiny tremors running through her body. So much for being prepared the next time she talked to him, she thought; so much for all the resolutions she had made in the dark of the night that he would not breach her defences again. She was falling in love with him, she knew she was, and she couldn't stop herself.

'It's good news about Tom's echocardiogram, isn't it?' she said, all brisk efficiency. 'I don't mean it's good news he has a hole in his heart,' she added, seeing his eyebrows rise, 'but it's good news that it should heal without the need for surgery.'

Sean gazed at her for a moment and then nodded. 'His parents are coming in later this afternoon for the results—do you want to tell them the news?'

She shook her head. 'That's your job.'

'You mean you actually trust me to do it properly?' he said quizzically.

'I do, surprising as it may seem,' she smiled, pushing open the swing doors and leading the way into Intensive Care before he could say any more.

'How's my favourite boy this morning?' she asked as she approached Christopher's bed.

He gazed up at her from the comic he was reading and smiled. 'I'm fine, Dr Abby.'

'How's his fluid intake, Sister Wilson?' she asked.

'He wasn't managing the 2.5 litres a day so Dr Ferguson is giving him the extra intravenously.'

'No sign of sickness, or increased temperature or pulse?'

Sister Wilson shook her head.

'You saved my life, didn't you?' Christopher commented. 'You and Dr Sean?'

'I don't know about that,' Abby smiled as she sounded his thin chest and took his temperature. 'All I remember is that you disturbed my beauty sleep.'

'There's no such thing,' he said stoutly. 'Either you're pretty or you're not, and you're pretty—isn't she, Dr Sean?'

'She is indeed, Christopher,' he replied. 'You see?' he added, glancing sideways across at her, his eyes warm. 'And that's a totally unbiased opinion.'

'My word, all these compliments.' Abby laughed shakily, annoyingly aware that her cheeks were reddening. 'If this goes on I'll get so big-headed I won't be able to get through the door!'

Christopher started to laugh and then broke into a paroxysm of coughing.

'Hey, no more laughing—and that's an order,' Sean said severely. 'Do you want to ruin all my handiwork?'

'Sorry,' Christopher gasped. 'I'll be better soon, won't I, and then we can go to Cawdor again as you promised?'

'Indeed you will,' Sean said encouragingly, though Abby noticed a slight frown on his forehead. 'Here's your mum and dad,' he added, noticing the couple coming towards them, 'so we'll leave you alone—but not too much excitement, promise?'

'Promise,' Christopher replied with a grin.

It was impossible to leave the ward without the Patersons thanking Sean profusely again for what he had done for their son. That Sean was acutely embarrassed by their praise was obvious. Occasionally he would glance in Abby's direction, his eyes saying all too clearly, For God's sake rescue me, but steadfastly she refused to come to his aid. He deserved the praise and she was sure it would do him good to see that his efforts were appreciated.

'Couldn't you have said a fire had broken out in the building, or someone had gone down with cholera?' he exclaimed, red-cheeked, when they had finally managed to extricate themselves from the Patersons.

'Enjoy it while you can,' she declared. 'By next week you'll be getting it in the neck from someone and this will be something pleasant to look back on.'

'I'd rather have the brickbats any day, thank you very much,' he said ruefully.

She gazed at him thoughtfully. 'You're the oddest man, Sean Maguire. The least bit of praise, the least compliment about your work, and you're as embarrassed as hell.'

'Hey, listen to who's talking,' he protested. 'You hate compliments as much as I do.'

'*Touché*,' she chuckled, and then her face grew serious. 'Something's worrying you about Christopher, isn't it?'

'The abscess doesn't seem to be draining as quickly as I'd hoped.'

'You think there may be some generalised peritonitis?' she said with concern.

'There are no other symptoms to indicate that and I really don't want to have to go in again unless it's absolutely necessary. Hey, don't look so worried,' he added bracingly as she paled visibly. 'I'm probably just worrying needlessly.'

She tried to smile and couldn't.

'Looking forward to our dinner tonight?' he continued, clearly deliberately changing the subject.

'Can't wait,' she said lightly.

The look on his face told her that he wasn't for one moment deceived, and quickly she walked away, all too conscious of his eyes boring into her back.

The rest of her shift was uneventful and time should have hung heavily on her hands but perversely the clock raced towards six o'clock and with no emergency to detain her she had to go home and get changed for the evening ahead.

A long, hot bath did nothing to ease her strained nerves; nor did a vigorous hair-wash which resulted in her curls being even more unruly than ever. Belligerently she stuck out her tongue at her reflection in the dressing-table mirror. She looked terrible. Too many disturbed nights had left dark shadows under her eyes and her wide cheekbones seemed all the more prominent, her chin all the squarer. Damn the man, she thought angrily. Damn him and his charm and his eyes which mocked and caressed and disturbed.

Why, oh, why had Robert asked Sean out to dinner with them? she wondered as she opened her wardrobe door. It wasn't as though they were friends—they hardly saw one another. The whole evening was going to be a disaster; she just knew it was. The only thing she had to be grateful for was that they weren't all travelling in the same car. She'd been insistent about that.

Half-heartedly she flicked through her clothes. On a normal date to the Rogano she wouldn't have thought twice. She'd have worn Robert's favourite dress—the black satin one. Then why should it be any different tonight? a little voice whispered, and deliberately she pulled it from its hanger and slipped it on.

The dress was calf-length with a wide full skirt and fitted strapless bodice on which dozens of tiny black seed-pearls gleamed and glistened. The starkness of the black should have drained any remaining colour she had but it didn't. Instead, her skin appeared creamy and translucent in contrast, her hair stood out like a flaming torch, and even the dark shadows under her eyes were no longer unflattering but added a strangely ethereal air.

Her reflection should have given her pleasure but didn't. Panic surged through her as she saw just how much of her cleavage the dress suddenly seemed to be revealing. She couldn't wear this, she thought, frantically tugging at the brief bodice in an attempt to hitch it higher. How in the world had she *ever* worn this?

Because you didn't think of your body when Robert

was taking you out, the mocking little voice whispered.

'Shut up, *shut up*,' she muttered through clenched teeth, and determinedly began to rifle through her wardrobe again, only to groan as the doorbell sounded. Trust Robert to be on time as usual. He couldn't have been late just for once.

'You're looking good, Abby,' he smiled as she opened the door.

'Actually I was just going to change into something else,' she replied. Something like a heavy tweed skirt, a shapeless sweater and a pair of flat brogues, she added mentally.

'We haven't the time,' he protested, glancing at his watch. 'We don't want to leave Carol too long on her own at the restaurant with just Sean to talk to.'

Oh, really, Abby thought as she pulled on her coat and followed him out to the car. Quite frankly she didn't give a damn right now if she and Robert never arrived at the Rogano.

'Sean's turning out to be an excellent chief of staff,' Robert observed as they drove out of the grounds of Ardmar and took the road leading to Inverness.

'I can't argue with that,' she replied evenly.

'I know how disappointed you were to lose out on the appointment, but you seem to be getting on well with him.'

'We have our ups and downs.'

Robert shot her a swift glance. 'Mostly ups, I think, and it must help that the two of you seem to share the same sense of humour.'

'I didn't know we did,' Abby replied, wondering just where this conversation was going.

'Carol finds him a bit daunting—she says she never knows where she is with him.'

Carol's not the only one, Abby thought, but said nothing.

'You like him—as a person, I mean—don't you?' Robert asked.

'Look, what is this?' she demanded, unnecessarily sharp. 'Have you nominated yourself Sean's PR man or something?'

'There's no need to get ratty,' he returned, equally terse. 'I know you didn't want me to organise this damn dinner and all I'm trying to say is that as you get on so well with the bloke it should be no big deal, all right?'

'Fine!' she snapped back and then sat, tight-lipped and silent, for the rest of the journey.

The proprietor of the Rogano recognised them immediately and came towards them with a beaming smile.

'So nice to see you again,' he enthused, taking Abby's coat. 'Still not married to this young man of yours, Doctor?' he added with a shake of his head, gazing pointedly at her left hand. 'He has the patience of Job, this fiancé of yours.'

Abby tried to join in Robert's laughter but it was not easy. She was as tense as a wire and the row with Robert hadn't helped—nor, indeed, did her very definite suspicion that things were only going to get worse.

'Carol looks relieved to see us,' Robert murmured as they made their way over to the table where Carol and Sean were already seated.

That was the understatement of the year. Carol looked like a desperate drowning woman who had just seen a lifeboat whereas Sean, by contrast, looked totally at ease. And why shouldn't he? Abby decided waspishly. If ever a man was born to wear a black dinner jacket, white dress shirt and black velvet bow-tie, it was Sean Maguire. Dressed in his white hospital coat he was extremely handsome, in evening wear he was totally devastating—a fact that had not escaped the attention of the other female diners.

All too unwillingly Abby found herself remembering dates she'd shared with Michael when similar admiring glances had come their way and deliberately she sat down next to Carol, leaving the vacant seat beside Sean for Robert.

'As Robert is kindly paying for this meal I think I should pay for the wine,' Sean declared. 'What about some champagne—make it a really special occasion?'

What about a nice cup of tea and we all go home? Abby's brain protested, but she smiled her agreement, seeing Carol and Robert's enthusiasm for the suggestion.

The champagne was good, the food was excellent; only the company could be faulted, Abby decided as the evening wore on. Sean didn't, as she had feared, spend the entire evening making veiled comments about the length of her engagement or the unsuitability of her choice. In fact he produced a fund of stories about his home town in Ireland which had Robert and Carol laughing and chattering away with him as if they'd known each other for years. Only she seemed on edge; only she couldn't relax.

'You're not eating much, Abby—are you feeling OK?' Sean asked during a lull in the conversation.

'I'm fine. I'm just not very hungry.'

'But I thought you told me once that you were the original dustbin?' he said.

She had, and the memory of what had happened after she'd told him was much too fresh in her mind for comfort.

'Abby's always had a healthy appetite, haven't you, sweetheart?' Robert said. 'You wouldn't believe what this girl can eat, Sean.'

'I've had personal experience of it, I'm afraid,' Sean

chuckled, and then bit his lip as what little colour there was drained rapidly from Abby's face. He hadn't intended to upset her, to remind her of a night she so clearly wanted to forget, but he'd done it nevertheless.

Luckily Robert didn't pick up on his comment, didn't ask when they'd shared a meal together. 'Is there something wrong with your meal, Abby?' he asked instead.

'It's lovely—really lovely,' she said quickly, forcing a couple of mouthfuls between her lips though her meal had all the appeal of ashes.

Robert seemed content with her reply and turned towards Carol but Sean's gaze stayed fixed on Abby.

She wasn't beautiful; she wasn't even pretty in the conventional sense. There were times when she drove him to distraction, times when he thought if he never saw her again it would be too soon, but increasingly there were times when he wanted her so badly it was a physical ache.

And he didn't just want to make love to her, he thought with surprise. Tonight, seeing how unhappy she was, he found himself wanting to do something quite ridiculous just to make her laugh, to ease her pain. A wry smile crossed his lips. What the hell was happening to him? It made no sense; no sense at all.

'Would you like to dance, Abby?' he asked.

Abby had seen the smile on his face and opened her mouth to refuse, but Robert answered for her.

'Go on, sweetheart,' he urged. 'You know what a lousy dancer I am, and I don't mind.'

And he truly didn't, she thought with a sigh as she got reluctantly to her feet.

'You're not enjoying yourself, are you?' Sean observed as he led her out onto the dance-floor.

She forced a smile to her lips. 'I'm having a wonderful time.'

'You're a rotten liar, Abby Hunter,' he commented,

drawing her into his arms as the band began to play.

'OK, so maybe I'm not at my best, but it's been a long week and I'm tired,' she replied.

'You're sure that's all it is?' he pressed, his eyes fixed on her.

'Yes, I'm sure,' she retorted. 'Look, I thought you wanted to dance, not subject me to an inquisition.'

'Fair enough,' he said mildly and then said no more.

He was finding it difficult enough anyway to concentrate on the steps he should be doing when he was all too aware of the tautness of her body under his hands, of the rapid rise and fall of her breasts under the black satin, and the startling whiteness of her skin against her red hair.

Once, by accident, her hair brushed lightly against his face, tantalising him with the sweetness of her perfume. And it was an accident. One glance at Abby's set face told him that but he couldn't resist gently drawing her closer to him, only to feel her pull back immediately.

'I won't stand on your toes,' he smiled, with a look that told her that he knew exactly why she'd moved away.

'Why did you accept Robert's invitation tonight?' she said tightly.

'Why should I have refused?' he countered.

Abby glanced up into his grey eyes and then away again quickly. How long would this dance go on? she wondered wretchedly. To have his arms around her was a form of exquisite torture. If it wouldn't have caused comment she would have walked off the dance-floor and left him standing there.

Sean sighed slightly. There was something he had to say to the girl in his arms, something he had been putting off for too long, and he supposed there was no time like the present. He cleared his throat. 'Carol and Robert—they make an attractive couple, don't they?'

Abby followed the direction of his gaze to see Carol and Robert deep in conversation about something, but it wasn't that that riveted her attention; it was the look on their faces as they gazed at one another. They're falling in love, she thought with a jolt of pain. They're falling in love and I hadn't even noticed.

'She'd be perfect for him, Abby,' Sean continued, as though he'd read her mind. 'She'll prop him up, tell him he's wonderful, whereas you'd steamroller right over the poor bloke.'

Her stomach tightened into a hard and painful knot. How long had he known, how long had he been laughing at her blindness, and how many others at Ardmar had been able to see what she hadn't? 'You don't have a very high opinion of me, do you?' she muttered.

'On the contrary, I have the very highest opinion,' he replied gently. 'Which is why I think you deserve someone considerably more worthy of you.'

It was the last thing she wanted to hear, and he was the last person she wanted sympathy from.

'Advice to the lovelorn now, is it?' she snapped. 'My, but you're a versatile man, aren't you?'

'Abby, listen—'

'No, you listen,' she flared. 'When I want your advice I'll ask for it, so butt out of my life, Sean!'

The music had stopped and she threaded her way thankfully through the other couples back to their table.

'You dance well together,' Robert observed with a smile as she sat down.

'I think any woman would dance well if she danced with Sean,' Abby said sweetly. 'What about you, Carol? I'm sure you'd like to dance with our chief of staff, wouldn't you?'

Carol looked as though she'd far rather be boiled in oil but obediently took Sean's reluctant hand and followed him out onto the dance-floor.

'You shouldn't have done that, Abby,' Robert chastised her as soon as they were alone. 'Carol was just telling me she never knows what to say to Sean—'

'I want to go home, Robert,' she said quickly. 'I'm not feeling very well—I've got this dreadful headache.'

It wasn't a lie. Her head was beginning to pound with the strain of the evening.

'But what about Carol?' he protested.

'What about Carol?' she replied more angrily than she'd intended. 'She can stay on here with Sean or they can go home too. Please, Robert,' she added as a deep frown appeared between his eyebrows. 'I really do feel wretched.'

'All right,' he said with clear reluctance. 'We'll tell them when they've finished their dance.'

'Can't we just go now—leave a message for them?' she urged.

'But it would be so rude!' he exclaimed.

She gritted her teeth, knowing that she didn't give a damn if she was breaking every single rule of social etiquette. 'They'll understand—I know they will,' she declared as evenly as she could. 'I want to go home, Robert, and I want to go home now.'

He sighed and nodded but the quick escape she longed for was not to be. By the time he had checked the bill, paid it, remembered the tip, and then called for her coat, Sean and Carol were back at the table.

'I'm afraid we're going to have to break up the evening early,' Robert said regretfully. 'Abby's not feeling very well.'

Carol murmured her sympathy but Sean, she noticed, said nothing.

'There's no need for the two of you to leave just

because we're going,' Robert continued. 'Why don't you stay on for a while?'

'Actually I'm a little tired myself,' Carol said quickly—too quickly.

There seemed little else to say. Carol's coat was called for, Sean settled the wine bill, and they made their way out into the street, which suddenly seemed oddly still and silent in comparison with the lively chatter and music of the restaurant.

'We must do this again some time,' Robert said jovially when they reached their cars.

Carol voiced her enthusiastic agreement and Abby said something but she didn't know what. All she was aware of was Sean's intent gaze, the compassion in his eyes, the compassion she couldn't bear.

She sat lost in silent thought during the long journey back to Ardmar but when Robert drew the car up outside her cottage she didn't get out. Instead she sat where she was, remembering the look on Carol's face as she'd gazed at Robert. She had never looked at him like that, not once in the two years they'd been engaged. She glanced across at Robert and cleared her throat.

'You don't want to marry me any more, do you, Robert?'

He didn't look at her for a long time and when he spoke his voice was barely audible. 'No.'

'It's Carol, isn't it?'

He turned towards her quickly, his face showing his surprise. 'How did you know?'

'I didn't—I should have done—but I didn't, not until tonight.'

'Abby, I'm sorry—truly sorry. . .'

'Don't be,' she said gently. 'If anyone is at fault it's me. I should never have accepted your proposal in the first place. I thought—well, it doesn't matter what I thought now. I'm just glad I had the sense not to marry you. You deserve a lot better than I can give you, Robert.'

'I'm still very fond of you, Abby,' he said awkwardly.

'I know you are,' she murmured, 'but it's not the same as what you feel for Carol, is it?'

He shook his head. She stared down at the blue sapphire surrounded by a cluster of diamonds sparkling on her hand in the moonlight and then deliberately pulled it off and handed it to him.

'Carol should be back in her flat by now,' she said. 'Why don't you go and see her?'

He reached across and kissed her on the cheek. 'You're a very special person, Abby.'

'I'm well-known for it,' she managed to reply. 'Now go on—get out of here before I change my mind.'

She stood outside her cottage for a long time after he'd driven away, letting the tears trickling slowly down her cheeks fall unchecked.

Was it always going to be like this? she wondered bleakly. Was she always going to choose the wrong man? The pain she felt inside wasn't the searing pain she'd experienced when Michael had told her he'd never loved her but there was pain nevertheless—the pain of rejection.

What am I going to do now? she wondered as she stared into the future and saw nothing there but a vacuum of loneliness. Robert had been a solid, dependable part of her life for so long and now she felt like a ship drifting without a rudder, a ship that had no destination, a ship that had no safe haven in sight. 'What do I do now?' she murmured out loud to the night sky, and the stars gleamed and shimmered down at her and said nothing.

CHAPTER SEVEN

IT TOOK just a day for the news of Abby's broken engagement to become common knowledge. One glimpse of her bare left hand was enough to set tongues wagging, and once she'd confirmed the situation to Molly Jordan the entire hospital knew by nightfall. Reactions varied from the frankly curious to embarrassing consolation, and Abby gritted her teeth and smiled and prayed that soon—please God, soon—some other piece of juicy gossip would surface to take the attention off her.

The only person who did not question her decision was the one person she had expected to. Sean didn't seek her out; if anything she would have sworn he was doing his level best to avoid her, but eventually, late one afternoon, just as she was beginning her evening rounds, she saw his tall figure advancing purposefully towards her.

'Something I can do for you?' she asked evenly.

'Molly tells me you've called off your engagement,' he said.

She stared up at him, trying to read his expression, but couldn't. 'Well, at least you're not hypocritical enough to say you're sorry,' she replied, tight-lipped. 'Are you happy now? Am I going to be allowed to run my own life in the future or are you still going to feel compelled to put in your penny's worth?'

He gazed at his hands for a moment and then back at her. 'Is that how it's felt?'

'Oh, come on, Sean,' she protested. 'You've done

nothing but stir it between Robert and me since the day you arrived.'

'Only with the best of intentions,' he declared defensively.

A wry smile appeared on her lips. 'What do they say—the road to hell is paved with good intentions?'

He looked at her for a long moment. 'You didn't keep your promise.'

'What promise?'

'That if you needed someone to talk to, a shoulder to cry on, you'd come to me.'

'I don't need to talk and I most certainly don't need a shoulder to cry on,' she said coolly. 'I'm fine.'

His glance took in her too large brown eyes set in a strained, chalk-white face and he shook his head. 'Far be it from me to call you a liar, but you look anything but fine to me.'

'Considering what you've called me in the past I'd say "liar" is pretty close to a compliment,' she retorted, sweeping past him into the ward, only to discover with annoyance that he had followed her.

'How's the gang, Kate?' she asked, deliberately ignoring him.

'Dr Bell admitted John-Robert this afternoon. It's another fracture, I'm afraid—his arm this time.'

Abby went over to the youngster's bed. 'Are you going for some sort of world record or what?' she teased.

'I wasn't doing anything stupid—honest,' John-Robert replied. 'I fell over my brother's toy tractor, that's all.'

'I think we should give serious consideration to trying another bone-marrow transplant, Abby,' Sean murmured.

'I'm quite well aware of the treatments available for

osteopetrosis, thank you, Dr Maguire,' she said through clenched teeth.

'I wasn't implying you didn't,' Sean replied, equally terse. 'All I meant was that it might be worth a third try.'

John-Robert glanced from Abby to Sean. 'Are you having a row? My mum and dad always look like that when they're having a row.'

'Doctors don't have rows, John-Robert,' Abby said evenly. 'They have professional disagreements.'

'Looks like a row to me,' John-Robert muttered, and Abby quickly moved on to the next bed, hoping that Sean might take the hint and leave, but he didn't.

He stayed with her throughout her rounds, never uttering a word, making no comment at all, until she was so taut she was ready to explode.

'Right, that's the lot,' she said when she had completed the medication charts. 'I'm going down to the canteen now for a cup of coffee, Sean—am I to be allowed to drink it on my own or do you feel the need to hold my hand there too?'

A faint flush of colour appeared on his cheeks but his voice when he spoke was even. 'Finlay Norris phoned yesterday—he's managed to persuade his friends in London to set up the trust fund for Ardmar.'

'Good.'

'It's going to be a big help financially.'

'I expect so,' she answered, making for the ward door.

'At the very least it should solve some of our more pressing financial problems,' he continued determinedly.

'I'm very glad to hear it.'

He thrust his hand through his black hair in defeat. 'Abby, this is crazy! I'll admit I didn't think Robert was right for you but why are you taking your anger out on me?'

The hurt she'd felt for the last four days boiled over. 'Why am I taking it out on you?' she said bitingly. 'I'm taking it out on you because you're no better than those so-called friends of mine at med school. All those sly little innuendos—he's not right for you, Abby; he's not good enough for you, Abby! You couldn't just have come right out and said it, could you? You couldn't just have told me that Robert was falling in love with Carol. Oh, no, you had to stand by and enjoy watching me making a complete fool of myself!'

She swung on her heel to walk away, only to find herself caught and then propelled in a vice-like grip into the empty sluice room.

'Let go of me!' she snapped as he pinned her hard against the wall with his hands.

'Not until you've heard what I have to say,' he replied, infuriatingly calm. 'Number one, I didn't know they *were* falling in love initially. All I knew was if you married him it would be a complete disaster. Number two, when I did find out, can you honestly say you'd have believed me if I'd said anything? And number three. . .' His eyes caught and held hers. 'Number three is that I was too much of a coward. I didn't want to be the one who told you; I didn't want to be the one who hurt you.'

There was compassion in his dark grey eyes—compassion and something else, something that made her heart turn over dizzily. She closed her eyes tightly and a small sob broke from her. 'You've said what you wanted to say; now let me go, Sean.'

'Only if you'll tell me you believe me,' he insisted.

'All right, I believe you,' she whispered, all too aware of his closeness, of the sheer masculine power

of him, and the emptiness of the sluice room. 'Now
please just go away.'

'Abby—'

'Please, Sean,' she said raggedly. 'I'm sure you mean
well, but please. . .please just go away now.'

'All right, acushla,' he murmured, releasing her with
a sigh that seemed to reach into her heart.

She waited until the sound of his footsteps had faded
into nothingness in the corridor outside before she
allowed her tears to flow. What had he called her—
acushla? It probably meant fool, idiot, in Irish—and
that's what I am, she thought wretchedly. I'm in love
with a man who could hurt me more than Michael
ever did.

When she had cried herself into an aching silence
she crept out of the sluice room and made her way
quickly to her office to repair her ravaged make-up as
best she could. There was something she had to do
before she went home for the night, one person she
had to see, and then maybe then—she could face the
world with something like normality.

She stared at her reflection in the mirror. She looked
pale but a touch of blusher helped that. As for her
eyes—well, they weren't too puffy, she thought. But
whether they were puffy or not was immaterial, she
decided as she squared her shoulders deliberately—
what she wanted to do couldn't wait.

The hospital canteen was as crowded as she had
hoped it would be but the first person she saw was
Jean Lawrie.

'I've been looking all over for you, my dear,' she
smiled. 'Come and sit with me for a minute.'

It wasn't what Abby wanted but she grabbed a cup
of coffee and obediently sat down.

'I've just heard the news—about you and Robert,'
Jean said in an undertone. 'You're making the right

decision, Abby. I never did think he was right for you.'

'I know—you told me,' Abby replied evenly.

Jean stirred her coffee. 'So you're footloose and fancy-free again?'

'That's right,' Abby said with an effort. 'Look out, world, here comes Abby Hunter.'

The coffee was stirred more vigorously. 'I can think of one man who'd suit you down to the ground, my dear.'

Abby didn't even have to ask who she meant. 'No, Jean.'

'But why not?' she protested. 'You like him—more than like him—'

'Liking is one thing, getting involved is something else.'

'The only trouble with Sean Maguire is he hasn't met his match yet,' Jean declared, 'and I think you're his match—more than his match.'

Abby shook her head. 'I've been there, done it, and got myself badly burned in the process. I've no desire to repeat the experience.'

'You're not talking about Robert, are you?' Jean said curiously.

'No, I'm not,' Abby said with a sad smile.

Jean sighed. 'So that's it, is it—you're throwing in the towel before you've even started?'

'There's nothing to start,' Abby replied, only to realise that a deadly hush had suddenly descended on the canteen.

She glanced round to see Carol standing by the counter with a cup of coffee in her hand, looking acutely uncomfortable. Deliberately Abby beckoned to her, only to feel Jean tugging at her sleeve, a look of clear consternation on her face.

'It's OK, Jean,' she said. 'I just want to make

something crystal-clear, that's all—though I would
appreciate a little privacy.'

Jean needed no second urging. With a backward
glance of concern she was gone.

Slowly Carol approached the table, embarrassment
plain in her large blue eyes.

'Sit down.' Abby smiled. 'I won't bite, I promise.'

Carol cleared her throat awkwardly, scarlet to the
roots of her blonde hair. 'Abby, I owe you an
apology—'

'No, you don't.'

'But you must hate my guts. . .'

'I was never right for Robert, Carol, and he was
never right for me.'

Carol gazed at her unhappily. 'I feel dreadful. You
and he were engaged. . .'

'Engaged, not married,' Abby said, pitching her
voice deliberately louder, well aware that every eye in
the canteen was watching them, every ear was strain-
ing, clearly hoping for a scene, a scene she had no
intention of providing. 'I wish the pair of you every
happiness—and I mean that from the bottom of
my heart.'

'Thank you,' Carol faltered in clear amazement.

Abby pushed back her chair. She'd done what she'd
intended to do—scotched any rumours that she and
Carol were at daggers drawn—and now all she wanted
was to go home.

'Good luck with the meeting,' Carol said as Abby
got to her feet.

'The meeting?' Abby echoed. 'What meeting?'

'Between Ben Reid and Dr Maguire. He was parking
his car as I came in and he told me he had a meeting at
seven o'clock with Dr Maguire to discuss his daughter's
future. I assumed—what with the interest you take in
Becky—that you'd be there.' Carol flushed deeply as

she saw Abby's blank face. 'Oh, boy, I've put my foot in it, haven't I? Dr Maguire hasn't told you, has he?'

'You're sure about this?' Abby said slowly, a frown appearing on her forehead. 'Ben definitely said the meeting was about Becky?'

Carol nodded. 'I don't know how Dr Maguire managed to persuade him to come in. . .'

The rest of what she'd been about to say died in her throat. She was already staring at Abby's retreating back as she made for the door.

Abby took the stairs at a run and arrived breathless and panting in Molly's office.

'Has Ben Reid arrived yet?' she demanded without preamble.

'We're just waiting for him—Abby—Abby, you can't just walk in—'

Oh, can't I? Abby thought as she strode into Sean's office, her colour high.

'Abby—what an unexpected surprise,' he declared, though he looked anything but pleased to see her. 'I thought you'd gone home.'

'Thought or hoped, Sean?' she said angrily. 'Why didn't you tell me you were seeing Ben Reid this evening? You know the interest I take in Becky—why all the secrecy?'

'I didn't tell you because I knew you wouldn't approve of what I'm going to do,' he said calmly.

The frown on her forehead deepened. 'Why wouldn't I approve—just what are you up to, Sean?'

'I'm going to make him face a few facts.'

There was something in the way he spoke that convinced her that wild horses wouldn't drag her from the room now.

'I have a right to be here,' she said firmly, 'and, unless you send for Security and have me thrown out, here I intend to stay.'

He shrugged. 'Suit yourself, but I warn you, Abby, I want no interference. We're playing things my way this time.'

'I won't say a word.'

A fleeting smile appeared on his face. 'I'm going to remind you of that promise later.'

It had been almost four months since Abby had last seen Ben Reid and she couldn't prevent the involuntary gasp that sprang to her lips when Molly ushered him in. Flecks of grey had appeared in his dark brown hair, his eyes were sunken, and judging by the tremor of his hands and the pallor of his skin Abby guessed that he was drinking more than was good for him.

If ever an occasion called for tact and gentleness this was surely such a time, but one look at Sean's set face told her it was likely to be a stormy interview and his opening words confirmed it.

'So you finally decided you could spare the time to come in and see us, did you, Mr Reid?'

A flush of angry colour swept across Ben's face. 'Considering you've been bombarding my answering machine with messages—'

'Most of which you've chosen to ignore,' Sean observed.

'Well, I'm here now,' Ben said defensively, 'so say what you want to say and let's get this over with.'

'What I want, Mr Reid,' Sean said, his voice cold, 'is to find out exactly what you intend to do about your daughter. She can't stay here—that much is certain.'

'This is a hospital, isn't it?' Ben countered.

'For sick children,' Sean replied. 'Becky isn't sick.'

Ben flinched. 'She is sick. She's—'

'She's paraplegic, which means she has no movement from the waist down and she's brain damaged, but she's not sick. She doesn't require hospitalisation any more than you or I do.'

Ben gazed across at Abby in desperation. 'This last year—it's been rough on me,' he faltered. 'I can't cope. . .'

'We do understand, Ben,' she said gently. 'No one is blaming you—'

'Mr Reid,' Sean broke in, 'if you'd seen some of the pathetic cases which have passed through my hands over the years you'd get down on your damn knees and thank God that paraplegia and slight brain damage are all that's wrong with your little girl.'

Ben shook his head. 'You don't understand—'

'I think I understand perfectly,' Sean retorted, his face hardening perceptibly. 'You want your perfect, beautiful child back again—that's it, isn't it? Well, it's not going to happen—not now, not ever!'

Anger flooded through Abby as Ben closed his eyes in pain. She'd said she wouldn't interfere but she couldn't just sit quietly and listen to Ben being put through the mill like this.

'I think you've said enough, Dr Maguire—'

'Oh, I've scarcely bloody well started,' he said grimly. 'We can't keep Becky here, Mr Reid,' he continued, turning back to him, 'and you don't want to take her home, so what are we supposed to do? Are we supposed to give your child a lethal injection, help you get her off your hands, is that it?'

'*Sean!*'

The horror in Abby's voice was plain but he ignored it, ignored her. 'You'd rather she'd died in the accident, wouldn't you, Mr Reid? Well, life's not that convenient, I'm afraid. With luck she'll have years ahead of her and you're stuck with her, Mr Reid— with the emphasis on the word *you*. We'll help you all we can, we'll treat any illnesses she falls prey to, we'll put you in touch with families who face similar problems, but we are not going to be a dustbin for you to dump your child in!'

Ben sprang to his feet, his fists clenched, his face white with fury. 'My God, but you're an insensitive bastard, Maguire!'

'A practical one, Mr Reid,' Sean said calmly. 'We have no room for a child who is not clinically ill. She's your child, your responsibility, and you've got to face it.'

'Call yourself a doctor?' Ben spat out, his voice rising in pitch. 'You don't give a damn about my daughter.'

'Do you?' Sean asked ironically.

'More than you do, it would seem!'

'Then prove it—face up to your responsibilities.'

Ben's face crumpled. 'It's all right for you—you can take the moral high ground—but you're not going to have to face what I'll have to face day after day for the rest of my life.'

Sean sighed. 'Mr Reid—Ben—I'm not saying it's going to be easy—it's not—but pretending you haven't got a daughter isn't the answer.'

Ben made for the office door. 'I don't know what to do,' he said, turning towards Abby, his voice choked with emotion. 'I can't think right now—I'll phone—come in again. But I can't think—not right now.'

The room was unnaturally silent after he'd gone. All that could be heard was the slow tick of the office clock as it crept its way towards half past seven and the steady tap of Molly's typewriter from the room outside. Slowly Abby got to her feet, her face almost as white as Ben's had been.

'Where are you going?' Sean said in surprise as she walked towards the door.

'Home,' she murmured. 'I've finished my shift for the day so I'm going home.'

'Aren't you going to say anything?' he asked, getting to his feet.

She glanced over her shoulder at him, her face an unreadable mask, and shook her head.

'Abby, wait!' he demanded, coming after her, only to collide with Molly as she brushed past Abby on the threshold.

'Could you sign these letters for me, Dr Maguire?' she said. 'They are urgent,' she added, seeing the exasperation on his face. 'Oh, and Dr Bell is here—he'd like a word.'

Sean listened to the sound of Abby's high heels growing fainter and fainter in the corridor outside and, with something suspiciously like an oath, tore the letters from a bemused Molly's outstretched hand and scrawled his signature over them.

Abby's cottage was quiet when she got home—too quiet. Deliberately she turned on the radio and then raided the freezer for something for her dinner though she wasn't in the least bit hungry. Keep busy, her mind said as she showered; keep busy and you won't have time to think. But eventually there was nothing left to do but wait for the frozen meal to cook and the thoughts she had been trying so desperately to crush down crowded and pushed their way into her mind.

How could he have done it? How could Sean have spoken to Ben as he had? She had seen Sean sarcastic, she had seen him unthinking, but she had never seen him deliberately cruel and he had been cruel—brutal. She pulled her bathrobe tighter to her and stared into the firelight. How could she have thought she was falling in love with this man? She didn't even know him.

The shrill jangle of her doorbell made her jump. She didn't want company—any company—and for a minute she debated ignoring it and then sighed. There could be an emergency, her phone might not be working, and reluctantly she went down the narrow corridor, only to discover when she opened the door that Sean was standing on the threshold, his face concerned.

'I'd like a word—'

The slamming of the door in his face was her only reply but he didn't take that for an answer. 'I want to talk to you,' he said, opening the door and coming in after her.

'Get out of my house!' she snapped.

'I want to talk to you.'

'Tough! Now get out of my house!'

She tried to walk on, but suddenly found herself pulled roughly round to face him. 'You're going to hear what I have to say whether you like it or not, Abby!'

She met him glare for glare and then shrugged herself out of his hands, her eyes cold. 'OK, say what you want to say and then get out.'

'Can I sit down?'

'Suit yourself.'

He didn't sit down. Instead he stood in the middle of the floor gazing at her.

'Is this going to take long?' she demanded, unaccountably unnerved by his silence. 'Only my dinner is in the oven—'

'Oh, for God's sake, Abby, shout at me, scream at me, tear me off a strip, but don't twitter on about your damn dinner!' he said, his voice harsh.

'What do you want me to say?' she said dully. 'That what you did to Ben was inexcusable? All right, then, I'll say it—it was inexcusable, totally inexcusable. There's making someone face the facts and there's crucifying them, and you crucified him, Sean.'

Suddenly he looked overwhelmingly weary. 'It had to be done.'

'And that salves your conscience, does it?' she said in disgust. 'I did it for his own good so to hell with how much I hurt him, to hell with caring if all I've done is land another guilt trip on him?'

'I've done rather more than that, I think.'

Her look was steady. 'Ben was right—you are an insensitive bastard. I thought you'd understand—I thought—after what you told me about your nephew—that you of all people would understand.'

'I do!' he exclaimed, raw pain clear in his eyes. 'I understand more than I'd ever want to. Oh, Abby,' he sighed, seeing her bewilderment, 'I won't ever forget that day I stood next to my sister and her husband listening to the clods of earth falling relentlessly onto Conor's coffin. If I could ask Sinead now which she'd prefer—to tend that little grave or to have Conor back again, to hold him in her arms, even if he was brain damaged and paraplegic—what do you think she'd say?'

She gazed at him silently. Perhaps he was right; perhaps, though the method had been brutal, Ben had needed to be faced with the facts. Her softly-softly approach hadn't worked, that was for sure.

'You're playing a hell of a dangerous game, Sean,' she murmured.

'I know,' he replied bleakly, and then turned as the timer from the kitchen bleeped insistently. 'I'd better go.'

'Would. . .would you like to join me for dinner— by way of a peace offering?' she said. 'There won't be a lot, but you're more than welcome to it—if you'd like,' she added hurriedly when he said nothing.

'I'd love to,' he said simply.

She went through to the kitchen wondering what

on earth had prompted her to make such an offer—
sympathy, perhaps, or loneliness, or was it something
she didn't even care to think about, far less put
into words?

They ate in virtual silence, both wrapped in their
own thoughts, but both increasingly aware of the spiral-
ling tension between them, and when Abby went to
make the coffee Sean followed her.

'Abby—'

'The kettle shouldn't take a minute,' she said, determinedly brisk. 'There's cheese and biscuits if you'd
like—'

'Abby.'

There was such softness in his voice, such entreaty,
that she would have had to be made of stone not to
turn round and look up at him, and she was not made
of stone.

He cupped her face in his hands, his lips curved into
an expression of exquisite tenderness. 'I want you,
Abby Hunter.'

She shook her head and tightened the knot on her
bathrobe. 'I don't play games, remember?'

'I'm not playing games!' he exclaimed. 'I want you
because I love you.'

'You can't,' she said uncertainly.

'Why can't I?'

'Because I'm not. . .because you're too. . . Oh, you
just wouldn't understand.'

'I won't if you don't ever finish a sentence,' he
smiled. 'What are you trying to say?'

'Can't we just talk about something else?' she muttered, turning to switch off the kettle.

'No,' he said. 'Why won't you believe me?' He
searched her face and saw the answer there. 'Stop it!'
he said harshly, his fingers digging so deeply into her
shoulders that she winced in pain. 'You are not to

compare me to Michael—do you hear me? You are not to look at me and see Michael!'

'I'm trying not to—I'm honestly trying not to,' she protested, and then could say no more because his mouth had come down on hers.

Her body quivered as his tongue slid inside her mouth and as he held her close and she felt him hardening a fire began to grow deep within her, a fire that spread and increased in intensity as his lips left hers and travelled down her throat.

Tell him to leave, her mind told her. Stop this now before it goes any further.

But I don't want him to stop, her heart and body sighed as he parted her bathrobe with his fingers and his mouth captured her nipples and teased them into an aching hardness. I don't want him to leave.

Where had all her resolve gone, her determination never to fall in love with a charming man again? she wondered as her body arched in response to the downward path of his gentle fingers. It had all gone—gone on the strength of a smile that lit up a dark face, a pair of grey eyes that caressed and admired.

She was reaching the point of no return and she knew it. Be rational, Abby; think straight, a warning voice whispered, but as she pulled back from him slightly he smiled down at her and suddenly being rational wasn't important any more. All she knew was that she wanted him, that she wanted the inevitable to happen, but there was something she had to tell him first.

'Do you remember what I said to you before—about baggy sweaters and hospital coats hiding a multitude of sins?' she said quickly. 'I wasn't joking.'

'Baggy sweaters?' he frowned.

'Oh, Sean, I wish I was slim, with a perfect figure, but I'm not. I have this little roll of fat around my midriff, and my hips and my thighs—they should be thinner too. . .'

He tilted her chin, a gentle smile on his face. 'I told you before I thought women should have curves where they're supposed to have curves and I meant it. Look, Abby,' he added softly, seeing the uncertainty in her face, 'if you don't want to do this, if you've changed your mind, just say so.'

'It isn't that,' she muttered.

'Then what is it? Tell me.'

She flushed. 'You'll laugh.'

'I won't ever laugh at you, acushla. What is it? What's wrong?'

She looked up into his eyes and then away again. She swallowed and stared fixedly at his chest. 'I've. . . I've never done this before.'

Silence was the only reply and she was forced at last to look up at him. His face was unbelievably tender. 'I'm not laughing, Abby.'

'But it's so stupid,' she protested. 'I'm thirty years old, for heaven's sake. People are jumping in and out of bed all over the place and at my age—not to have ever—it's so stupid.'

'I don't think it's stupid,' he murmured.

'Michael wanted me to—I don't know what made me say no; perhaps an inner voice was warning me not to trust him completely.'

'And Robert?'

Her colour deepened. 'He didn't pressurise me so I kept putting off the evil hour.'

A slight frown appeared on his face. 'Is that how you see making love—as some awful endurance test? If it is, sweetheart, then I won't pressurise you either; I can wait—'

'I don't want to wait any more,' she said quickly. 'It's just the longer I. . .I haven't, the more of a hurdle it's become in my mind. I'm so afraid, you see, of being as hopeless at making love as I am at relationships.'

'Everyone has to start somewhere,' he said tenderly.

'I know, I know, but for me—making love—it's like. . .it's like I'm a novice ice-skater and suddenly I'm being asked to compete in the Olympic Games.'

'An ice-skater in the Olympic Games?' he repeated, puzzled.

'Do you remember Torvill and Dean—when the judges held up straight sixes at the end of their performances?'

He nodded.

'Well, I have this recurring nightmare that after. . .after I've made love to someone they hold up twos—or even worse—for my performance.'

A deep, throaty chuckle came from him. 'Oh, Abby, I'm not laughing at you,' he said as she flushed crimson. 'Ye gods, if I'd known making love was judged like an Olympic event I don't think I would ever have done it either!' And as she started to laugh he held out his hand and she took it and led him into her bedroom.

Biologically she had known what to expect but never had she thought that it would be like this—that not only would her own body respond so readily to the slightest touch of his hands and mouth but that she would also want to touch him, to explore him.

Shyly at first and then with increasing wonder she ran her fingers over his muscular body, explored him with her lips, revelling in the gasps of pleasure he gave. She guessed, despite her total lack of experience, that he was letting her set the pace and loved him all the more for it so that when she finally opened herself to him she did so willingly, joyously.

And when he moved within her and her cry of ecstasy matched his own she knew she had found the one man she wanted to share the rest of her life with, the one man she truly loved.

When she woke some time later dawn was streaming through the curtains and she turned quickly, remembering, stretching out her hand for him. The space beside her was empty but a note was pinned to the pillow and she picked it up hastily.

> Decided it would not be a good idea if my car was seen outside your cottage in the early hours of the morning—Molly Jordan would have a field-day! Can't wait to see you again—all of you!
>
> Sean
>
> P.S. The judge never lies!

The judge never lies? She shook her head and pulled herself upright with a slight frown, only to notice that tiny pieces of paper were sellotaped to the bottom of the bed. She leant forward curiously and then a ripple of laughter came from her.

Written on every piece of paper was the number six.

CHAPTER EIGHT

ABBY drove to work that morning wrapped in a warm glow of happiness. So what if the rain was bouncing off her windscreen? So what if her hair was soaked by the time she'd made the quick dash from the car park to the hospital? For the first time in her life she felt alive and supremely happy.

'Great weather for ducks, eh, Doctor?' Fred, the maintenance man, said gloomily as she shook her hair out of her eyes and dripped water all over the entrance hall in the process. 'That's our summer over for this year—it will be winter before you know it.'

'I like winter, Fred,' she beamed. 'Big log fires, stodgy puddings, holly and Christmas-time.'

'Slush and freezing pipes—that's what winter is, Doctor,' he replied with a shake of his head, and Abby laughed and went up to her office to change into her white coat with a song on her lips.

Not even the news that Joe Ferguson had called in sick dampened her spirits as she started her morning rounds. Sean loves me, an inner voice kept repeating over and over again, and every time she heard it she started to smile.

'Hi there, Abby,' Sister Mackay said wearily as she came into Ward 3. 'You look bright and cheerful this morning—what's up?'

'Nothing special,' she replied lightly. 'I just got up this morning feeling great, that's all.'

'Well, whatever you're on can I have some, please?' Joan sighed.

'Are you OK, Joan?' Abby asked, noting the

136

extreme whiteness of her skin and the slight beading of sweat on her forehead.

'I've felt better,' she admitted. 'There must be some flu bug going round. Two of the student nurses phoned in sick this morning.'

'Dr Ferguson's off too,' Abby said with a slight frown. 'How are you going to manage—without the student nurses, I mean? Do you want me to ask Molly to phone the agency?'

Joan shook her head. 'I've done that already—the agency nurses should be here by lunchtime.'

Privately Abby didn't think Joan Mackay looked as though she'd make it until her coffee-break but she said nothing. An outbreak of flu was all they needed when practically every bed in the hospital was full.

'When did Craig Lattimer come in?' she asked curiously, recognising the fourteen-year-old.

'Dr Bell admitted him during the night,' Joan replied. 'Apparently he's been a bit bronchial for a couple of days and his parents thought they'd better bring him in to be on the safe side.'

Abby nodded. Craig's form of muscular dystrophy was the commonest, the Duchenne type, which occurred almost exclusively in boys. For years his family had refused to accept the fact, attributing his slowness in walking and his difficulty in climbing stairs to laziness, but now that he'd been in a wheelchair for three years his family were having to come to terms with the knowledge that not only did he have the disease but he would probably die in his twenties through respiratory or heart problems.

'What did Dr Bell diagnose when he admitted him?' she asked.

'Inflammation of the bronchial tubes,' Joan declared. 'He reckoned some antibiotics and a few days' bed-rest should do the trick.'

Abby uncurled her stethoscope. It would do no harm to check him herself.

'How are you feeling, Craig?' she said as she unbuttoned his pyjama jacket.

'Much too old to be in a damn kids' ward,' he wheezed crossly.

'Sorry about that,' she smiled as she listened carefully to his lungs and heart. 'Any pain when you breathe?'

'A little when I cough.'

Alastair Bell had been right. She could hear the characteristic whistling sound of inflamed bronchial tubes when Craig breathed out but the breath sounds were of the same duration so there was no sign of pneumonia in his lung.

'Well, I don't think you'll have to suffer the kids' ward for too long,' she told him. 'A few days and you should be able to go home.'

'Where's Dr Sean?' he asked, waving her hands away impatiently as she tried to rebutton his jacket.

'In his office, I should imagine,' she said, fighting to keep a tell-tale blush from her cheeks.

'He's not a bad old bloke for a quack,' Craig observed airily.

'Agreed,' she replied solemnly, and moved quickly on to the rest of the patients, only just choking down her laughter as she pictured Sean's face when she told him what Craig had said.

The rest of the morning sped by. Having Joe Ferguson's duties to do as well as her own meant that she had only completed half of the ward rounds by lunchtime but though her time was at a premium she knew she couldn't wait any longer. The need to see Sean was overwhelming and quickly she made her way up the stairs and along the corridor, a secret smile on her lips, a smile that was still there when she turned the corner and came to a dead halt.

For a second her brain refused to take in what she was witnessing. This isn't happening, she told herself; this can't be happening, not after last night. But it was. Sean was standing in the middle of the corridor with his arms wrapped round Carol. He was murmuring something to her and she was whispering something back and then to Abby's complete shock Carol stretched up and kissed him and he didn't draw back; he returned the kiss.

She didn't wait to see any more; she couldn't bear to see any more. Blindly she groped for the nearest door and practically fell into the laundry room.

She gripped the wooden shelving tightly, fighting the wave of nausea that flooded over her. It was happening to her again; it was Michael all over again. She dug her fingernails deep into the shelves until they hurt. How long had it been since they'd made love? Fourteen hours—less—and yet already he was working on Carol. Dear God, what was he trying to prove—that no woman was immune to his charm?

A low moan of pain came from her as she imagined that caressing, insidious voice, that voice she had been stupid enough to trust, whispering, 'Robert's not right for you, Carol; he's not good enough for you, Carol'.

God, she'd been such a fool, such a blind, stupid fool, but her stupidity ended here. She took a deep ragged breath that ended on a sob. There would be no confrontation this time as there had been with Michael, no demand for an explanation, no ugly, humiliating scene. If she'd learned one thing from the past it was that Sean was never going to know how much she cared; he was never going to know how much he had hurt her.

The corridor was empty when she came out and the temptation to bolt, to run for home, was strong. She moistened her lips shakily. Brazen it out, Abby, she told herself. Show him last night didn't mean a damn thing.

A treacherous tear coursed down her cheek as the memory of his muscular body holding her close came into her mind and she brushed it away angrily. Tears were what the old Abby Hunter would have shed; tears were for losers.

'You OK, Abby?' Kate Johnson said as she swung into Ward 1.

'Fine.'

'You look a bit green round the gills,' Kate observed. 'Not going down with this flu bug, I hope?'

'I'm perfectly fine, thanks,' Abby replied more curtly than she'd intended and walking smartly across to John-Robert's bed. 'How's our most accident-prone patient today?'

Kate laughed. 'Do you want the good news or the bad news?'

'Good news first—I could do with some today,' Abby replied feelingly.

'Well, the good news is his fracture's healing well. Now do you want to tell the doctor the bad news, John-Robert, or will I?' Kate asked, her face severe but her eyes twinkling.

John-Robert grinned. 'It's just a joke, Staff Nurse Kate.'

She shook her head. 'I don't think Dr Abby is going to think it's a joke, my boy.'

'Dr Sean laughed when he saw it,' John-Robert replied defensively though the confidence in his eyes wavered slightly as he saw Abby's eyebrows snap down.

'Dr Sean?' she queried. 'What has this got to do with Dr Sean?'

'Show Dr Abby what you've done, John-Robert,' Kate ordered.

Reluctantly he drew his plastered arm out from under the bedclothes and hot colour swept across Abby's face. The child had drawn a large red heart in Biro on his plaster, a large red heart pierced with an arrow beside which two sets of initials stood out all too clearly—A. H. and S. M.

'Dr Sean thought it was funny,' John-Robert murmured, glancing up at her uncertainly. 'And then he said I must have the second sight and gave me a one-pound coin—See,' he added, pulling it out of his pyjama jacket. 'What's second sight, Dr Abby?'

She ignored the question. 'Can it be erased, Kate—the heart and the initials?' she said tightly.

'I'm afraid ink's the very devil—'

'Then I want those initials made illegible—and I want them made illegible *now*!'

Kate shot her a quick glance and took her pen and scribbled over the initials. 'He didn't mean any harm, Abby,' she said in an undertone as she followed her to the next bed. 'It was just a joke—'

'Which doesn't appeal to my sense of humour,' Abby retorted.

Kate frowned slightly and threw a backward glance of encouragement at John-Robert, who was looking decidedly glum.

'Dr Maguire said he'd like a word with you when you can spare the time,' Kate said.

'Did he say what he wanted?' Abby asked, mechanically examining the child in front of her.

'Just that he wanted a word. I don't think he's gunning for you or anything—in fact I'd say he was full of the joys today for some reason.'

Oh, I'll just bet he is, Abby thought savagely. I'll bet he's swanning round the hospital with a look of smug self-satisfaction on his face. No wonder he found John-Robert's heart funny—it boosted his ego and made me look ridiculous in one fell swoop.

She completed her visit to Ward 1 in almost total silence, reserving her conversation solely for the children, and made for the door well aware that Kate Johnson's eyes were following her with open curiosity. She was going to have to lighten up; she knew that. If she carried on like this tongues would start to wag but it was so hard to appear carefree and light-hearted when there seemed to be a large weight pressing on her chest, crushing it.

'Abby!'

Her heart lurched violently but deliberately she steeled herself as Sean came down the passage towards her, a blinding smile on his face.

'I can't stop, Sean. Joe Ferguson's called in sick and I'm having to do his shift today as well as my own.' How calm she sounded, she thought in surprise; how controlled.

'I didn't have the opportunity to say good morning when I left so I'd rather like to do it now,' he murmured, lifting her chin towards him only to see her jerk away quickly.

'I'm behind schedule—'

'Hey, wait up there,' he protested as she started to walk on. 'You did get my note, didn't you?'

'Yes, I got your note—now can I go, please?' she said, gazing pointedly down at his hand on her arm.

He took his hand away slowly. 'Is there something wrong, Abby?'

God, he was good, she thought dispassionately. Just the right amount of concern combined with ingenuous bewilderment.

'What could be wrong?' she said.

'I thought—after last night. . .'

'You thought what, Sean?' she said coolly.

He thrust his hand through his hair—an action that her traitorous heart found overwhelmingly appealing. 'I thought what we shared was special. I thought, I believed, you cared for me.'

'Did you?' she said, her gaze blank.

'Abby, what is this?' he asked slowly, his eyes narrowing. 'We slept together, in case you've forgotten. We can't just pretend it didn't happen—I sure as hell don't want to pretend it didn't happen.'

She dug her clenched fists deep into the pockets of her white coat. 'Last night was last night, Sean. Today's another day and what happened—it's over, done with, finished.'

'But why?' he protested. 'Did I hurt you? Did I do something you didn't like? Talk to me, Abby. I thought we had something—'

'We did—we had a good time,' she said evenly. 'But that's it, end of story.'

'I don't believe you mean that.' His voice was harsh. 'I *won't* believe you mean that.'

She met his gaze with a level stare. There was hurt in his grey eyes, confusion, disbelief, and for a second she almost found herself believing he truly cared, and then she remembered Carol—Carol locked in his arms, Carol who was being deceived just as she had been.

'So you're a mind-reader now, are you?' She laughed brittlely, though the hard lump in her stomach made her feel quite ill. 'Last night, we. . .we made love.' She stumbled over the words. 'But that doesn't mean you own me, or have exclusive rights to me— nobody does.'

'But Abby—'

'Chalk it up to experience, Sean,' she said, her voice light, indifferent. 'That's what I'm going to do.'

She didn't wait for his reply. She walked smartly down the corridor, her shoulders straight, her head thrown back, and told herself over and over again, I am not going to cry, I am *not* going to cry.

For the next few days she threw herself into her work, hoping to make herself so tired by the end of the day that sleep would come easily to her. It didn't work. As soon as she crawled into bed the memory of Sean's hands touching her, arousing her would rise up to taunt and mock her and she would toss and turn and get up the next morning no more refreshed than when she'd gone to bed.

Even the single piece of good news she received was tinged with bitter irony. Christopher Paterson had finally been pronounced fit enough to be moved out of Intensive Care but to her acute dismay there was only one vacant bed in the hospital and that was in Ward 6—Carol Lennox's ward.

She had been making her visits there as brief as possible, talking to Carol as little as she decently could, but Christopher's small face lit up with such pleasure whenever he saw her, and he so wanted to talk, that she was forced to linger even though Carol's presence stretched her self-control to the very limit.

'Look, Abby,' Carol said uncertainly late one afternoon. 'You would tell me, wouldn't you, if I'd done something to annoy you?'

Abby gazed at the girl's white, strained face, at the dark shadows ringing her large blue eyes. Carol looked almost as bad as she did.

'Of course I would,' she replied with a superhuman effort at a smile. 'If I've seemed a bit. . .tense lately it's just that I'm tired—these double shifts are really taking it out of me.'

Carol nodded and a surge of bitter anger flooded through Abby, anger that was directed solely at Sean.

Why couldn't he have left Carol alone? Why couldn't he just have accepted that she was in love with Robert? And she had been in love with him until Sean had started to confuse and bewilder her. For a second she was tempted to tell the girl what a louse Sean was but she didn't. Carol would never believe her. She doubted if she would have if someone had said the same thing to her.

'There's just one thing before you go,' Carol continued as Abby completed her medication charts. 'Christopher Paterson—it's probably nothing to worry about but his temperature's gone up a little.'

'How much is a little?' Abby asked quickly.

'Just a degree—nothing major—and he seems fine apart from that. He had his dinner last night and lunch today but I thought I'd just mention it. Becky Reid's the same—her temperature's gone up too.'

Abby frowned. She had been hearing the same story in the other wards for the last two days. Some children's temperatures had gone up inexplicably and a couple had been sick. Sean had sent samples to the local health authority just to be on the safe side but it looked as though the flu bug was hitting the children now.

'Have either Christopher or Becky been sick at all?' she asked.

Carol shook her head. 'Both of them seem quite fit apart from this slight temperature rise.'

'Right, I want both their temperatures taken every hour, on the hour,' Abby said firmly. 'The least change—even if it's only a degree—call me at once.'

'Should I tell Dr Maguire?'

You can tell him to go to hell for all I care, Abby thought but managed to mutter her agreement.

The situation was impossible, she thought wearily as she made her way to her office. She couldn't carry on like this; she couldn't go on working here with Sean, feeling as she did about him. And how do you feel about him? a little voice whispered. I still love him, her heart cried. Despite everything I'm still stupid enough to love him.

Despondently she opened her office door—and stopped dead on the threshold. Sean was sitting on the edge of her desk, reading one of her medical books. With a cursory nod in his direction she picked up a sheaf of case-notes and turned on her heel to go out again, only to find herself being pulled backwards in a tight, hard grip and the door slammed shut.

'All right, I've taken about as much of this as I can stand, Abby Hunter,' he said grimly. 'It's time for some straight talking.'

Not a muscle moved on her face. 'If you have a case you wish to discuss with me then I can spare you a few minutes, otherwise—'

'You can't keep on avoiding me, Abby.'

It was true—that was exactly what she'd been doing—but she wasn't going to let him get away with believing it for a minute. Her lip curled.

'My God, but you've got some ego, haven't you?' she said bitingly. 'The reason you've seen so little of me couldn't possibly have anything to do with the fact that the staff are going down like ninepins with this bug and I'm running from one ward to the next trying to keep up, could it? No, of course it couldn't. It all has to be all down to you, doesn't it?'

His face darkened. 'OK, that takes care of your working hours. How about explaining why you don't ever reply to any of the messages I leave on your answering machine, why you pretend to be out each time I call at your house?'

She swallowed hard and tried to calm her thudding heart. 'Simple answer, Sean—I prefer to keep my personal and my professional life separate.'

Baffled anger and frustration flitted across his face. 'What have I done that's made you shut me out like this?' he cried. 'You're driving me crazy—you know that, don't you?'

He looked totally drained and for a second she was almost tempted to take him in her arms, to soothe and comfort him, and then unbidden and unwanted a picture came into her mind, a picture of Carol's blonde hair lying across his broad chest, of Carol's lips receiving the kisses she had received. Anger and pain and hurt welled within her as she realised it probably didn't need two guesses to figure out why he looked tired and unconsciously her face set.

'Is that it—have you finished?' she demanded.

His expression hardened. 'Not quite.'

He jerked her towards him with such force that the case-notes in her hands fell to the floor and then his mouth came down on hers. She tried to struggle free but his hold on her arms only tightened as his lips forced hers apart in a kiss that both hurt and aroused at the same time. Her mind told her body not to respond but her body was not listening to her mind and she found herself returning his kisses with a desperate, hopeless intensity.

Desire raced through her as his hands caressed her breasts into an aching hardness through the sheer silk of her blouse and an involuntary moan escaped her lips, a moan that was cut off as he forced her chin up.

'Now tell me you don't want me as much as I want you,' he demanded, his breathing as ragged as hers. 'Now tell me what we had is over, finished!'

There was a look of triumph on his face and a small sob of self-disgust broke from her at having reacted exactly in the way he had wanted.

'God, how I hate you,' she whispered. 'I don't think

I've ever hated another human being as much as I hate you right at this minute!'

His face twisted and his hands fell to his sides in a gesture of defeat and shakily she bent to retrieve the scattered case-notes, fighting to regain her self-control.

'I'm sorry, Abby,' he said flatly. 'I thought. . .I hoped. . .' He shook his head. 'I don't know what it is about you but somehow you seem to bring out the best and the worst in me.'

'There's a difference?' she said icily.

'Oh, acushla—'

A firm knock on the door silenced him.

'Come in,' Abby called deliberately, and saw Jean's head pop round the door.

'Busy, my dear?' she said, glancing from Abby's flushed face to Sean's white one.

'Afraid so,' Abby replied, amazed at how even her voice sounded when her heart was doing uncomfortable somersaults in her breast. 'If it's me you want to see I won't be free until around five o'clock.'

'Perhaps Sean could entertain me for a while?' Jean suggested with a smile.

'I've no doubt he could,' Abby replied coolly. 'Sean's very good. . .at entertaining.'

Jean waited until Abby had gone and then gazed at Sean's tight face. 'I seem to have come at a bad time.'

'There are no good times as far as Abby and I are concerned any more,' he said pensively, bending down to retrieve a folder Abby had overlooked.

Jean sat down. 'OK—give. What's going on—have the two of you had some sort of row?'

'I wish we had—it would make life easier to understand,' he sighed, sitting down at Abby's desk. 'You're her friend, Jean. Will you speak to her for me, try and find out what I've done or said that's so upset her?'

'Why don't you ask her yourself?'

His lips tightened. 'The only questions she'll answer from me are those concerning the patients or Ardmar. If I try and ask her about anything else it's like talking to the wall.'

Jean sighed. 'You can't expect to be her favourite person at the moment, Sean. You were the one who told her Robert wasn't the right man for her and no one likes the idea that someone else was right and they were wrong—it smacks too much of "I told you so".'

'That isn't why she's not talking to me,' he murmured.

'Then why isn't she?'

Sean said nothing and Jean rolled her eyes heavenwards in exasperation.

'We're not running a friendship agency at Ardmar, you know,' she declared. 'This is a workplace. As long as Abby's doing her work efficiently, if she isn't being downright rude or obstructive, does it matter a hill of beans that you're not the greatest chums in the world?'

He spread his hands on the table. 'The trouble is I don't want her to be just a colleague, Jean. I want. . .I care about her.'

Jean leant forward in her seat, her eyes alight. 'Do you mean care as in "care to dance", care as in "I don't care", or care as in "I love her"?'

'Care as in I love her.'

A wide smile of triumph appeared on Jean's face. 'Could you repeat that a little louder, please, just in case I may have misheard you?'

He grinned ruefully. 'I love her, Jean. I don't know why; I don't even know how it happened; I just know that it has and she won't even give me the time of day.'

'I warned you you were playing with fire, didn't I?' she said, shaking her head. 'I warned you you'd get your comeuppance one day.'

'I need your help, Jean, not a sermon,' he protested.

She sighed. 'What do you want me to do?'

'Find out why she's shutting me out like this. Find out what I've done or said that's made her hate me so.'

She stared at him. 'It's got that bad between you?'

'It's got that bad, yes.'

'OK, I'll do my best,' Jean replied, 'but I can't promise anything.' And Sean had to be content with that.

Abby had totally forgotten about Jean by the time she came back to her office after she'd finished her shift and her heart sank when she found her leafing through an old magazine, waiting for her.

'You look dreadful, my dear,' Jean said, gazing at her critically.

'I'm not surprised,' Abby replied evenly. 'We're all working at full stretch at the moment. Which is why, if you don't mind,' she added as she hung up her white coat, 'I'd like to forgo our chat tonight—I'm really bushed.'

'You and Sean.'

Abby smoothed down the folds of the coat. 'What about me and Sean?'

'Did you know that William was forty years old when I met and married him?' Jean observed. 'The poor lamb thought he was making all the running—men generally do think that, you know, my dear—but he didn't stand a cat in hell's chance. I took one look and thought, That's the man for me.'

'I thought we were talking about Sean,' Abby said, walking quickly over to her desk and beginning to tidy the folders on it.

'I am—indirectly,' Jean said, her eyes fixed on Abby's face. 'Lots of men think they're confirmed bachelors until they fall in love.'

'*Love*?' Abby's voice was like a whiplash. 'Sean

Maguire wouldn't know the meaning of the word! I wish to God he'd never come here, Jean. I wish he'd never applied for the post. If he hadn't it would have been mine and none. . .none of this would ever have happened.'

Jean stared at the floor, acute embarrassment plain on her face. 'I'm afraid even if Sean hadn't applied for the post you wouldn't have been appointed, my dear. William told the board privately just before he died that he couldn't recommend you to succeed him.'

'I don't believe you,' Abby said uncertainly. 'William wouldn't have done that. He always said I was one of the best doctors Ardmar ever had—'

'And so you are, but William was afraid your life was becoming too narrow, too focused.'

'Since when did dedication become a demerit?' Abby demanded.

'It isn't,' Jean replied simply. 'Not so long as that dedication's balanced by something—or someone—else in your life. If it isn't, it's all too easy to develop tunnel vision, to become judgemental and hard.'

'William thought I was judgemental and hard?' Abby said in horror.

'He thought that was how you might *become* if you were appointed,' Jean said quickly. 'He thought—oh, this is so very difficult to phrase without hurting you,' she added. 'He thought that as chief of staff, with no one on the premises strong enough to stand up to you, you might lose the human touch.'

Abby gazed at her bleakly. Her whole world was falling apart. She'd lost Sean and Robert. What was more, the one thing that had remained constant was her conviction that she was good at her job and now she was being told she wasn't.

'I should resign, shouldn't I?' she murmured.

'Absolutely not!' Jean declared vehemently. 'I

wouldn't have told you any of this if I'd known this was how you were going to react and I'm talking about the past—about the Abby of the past. You're not the same girl now, not since knowing Sean.'

'Don't I just know it.' Abby's laugh was bitter.

'Sean asked me to speak to you—'

Abby's eyes flashed. 'He had no right. He got what he wanted from me—what does he want now—blood?'

Jean sighed. 'Look, I don't know what's been going on between the two of you—and I don't want to know. All I do know is he told me he loves you and I believe him.'

Something almost like a snort came from Abby. 'So he's got you fooled too, has he?' she said tightly. 'I've got to hand it to him—he can be very convincing when he wants to be.'

Jean stared at her in confusion. 'Why are you doing this to yourself? If you'd had a row—'

'A *row*?' Abby's face twisted slightly. 'Oh, Jean, if you only knew the half of it.'

'Then put it right, sort it out, before you lose the best thing that's ever happened to you. If he's in the wrong forgive him, if you're in the wrong then swallow your pride and apologise, but do *something*!'

'I'm doing it now—treating him with the contempt he so richly deserves!' Abby snapped back.

'But Abby—'

'I don't want to talk about him any more, Jean.'

'You're making a mistake, you know.'

Abby shook her head. 'I made one—past tense—and I have no intention of making another one. And now, if you'll excuse me, I'm going home.'

She didn't wait for Jean's reply. She simply tugged her coat from the hanger and went.

The rain that had been falling steadily for over a week now was still showing no sign of letting up as she made a quick dash from the hospital steps to her car, skirting the many deep puddles in the gravel as best she could. Shivering slightly, she opened her car door, but before she could get in she saw Sean's tall figure running down the steps towards her and a decidedly unladylike oath sprang to her lips.

'Abby—'

'Look, Sean, we've got nothing to say to one another—'

'We've got trouble,' he said, cutting her short abruptly.

She was all attention immediately, her animosity towards him temporarily forgotten. 'Is it one of the children?'

'The health authority's just rung. You remember I sent samples to them from the children who have been sick just to be on the safe side?'

She nodded.

'Their lab has just got back to us. We haven't got a flu bug, Abby. The hospital's got an outbreak of Campylobacter—one of the most virulent forms of food poisoning there is.'

CHAPTER NINE

ABBY drew her car to a skidding halt in the middle of the driveway and stared in blank amazement at the crowd of people gathered on the front steps of the hospital. She'd only gone home for a couple of hours to shower and change and Ardmar looked as though it was suddenly under siege.

'It's the Press, I'm afraid, Dr Hunter,' one of the gardeners declared, walking over to her car. 'They must have got wind of the outbreak and they all arrived about half an hour ago. Bloody ghouls, that's what they are.'

Abby groaned. 'Any chance I can get in round the back without having to go through that lot, Bob?'

He shook his head. 'Dr Maguire's had the back doors locked—you can get out from the inside but not in from the outside, if you know what I mean. He caught a couple of photographers trying to sneak in earlier—probably trying to take some pictures of the kids.'

'Hell and damnation,' she muttered.

'You said it, Doc,' Bob sighed, rubbing his weather-beaten chin with his hand. 'Mind you, it's the parents I feel sorriest for. They're worried enough without having to run the gauntlet of that load of vultures this morning.'

Abby nodded, let out her clutch, and began to crawl her way towards the front of the building.

The last three days had been a nightmare. The health authority had sent a team of specialists to Ardmar to take samples from the kitchens and to subject all of the medical and ancillary staff to a rigorous medical

examination in case one of them should be an unsus-
pecting carrier of the infection, but as yet they had
come up with no positive findings.

Campylobacter outbreaks were dangerous enough in
any hospital where patients' defences were low due to
illness but in hospitals for children and the elderly they
were particularly serious and everyone knew it was
vital that the source be discovered quickly.

Any hope Abby might have had that she would be
able to get into the hospital without being questioned
was quickly dashed. As soon as she got out of
her car she was engulfed in a sea of pushing, jostling
photographers and reporters.

'Has the source of the outbreak been traced yet, Dr
Hunter?'

'Is it true some of the children are near to death?'

'Will the hospital have to close?'

'Is there any truth in the rumour that it isn't
Campylobacter at all but typhoid?'

'No, of course it isn't typhoid!' she retorted angrily,
putting a hand up to her face to shield her eyes from
the glare of the cameras' flash lights. 'Look, any news
about the situation will be issued through official
channels. I've no comment to make—none whatso-
ever—so will you all just get out of my way before I
call for Security?'

'Is it true the board of governors are calling for Dr
Maguire's resignation?' someone demanded, thrusting
a microphone under her chin.

'That's utter rubbish,' she flared. 'The board have
complete trust in him—'

'Then why are they holding an emergency meeting
here tomorrow?'

She turned round to face the reporter, her face showing her surprise. 'Who told you that?'

'George Benson—owner of Benson's Farm Fresh Chickens.'

It would be him, she thought with anger. What did it matter if some of the children were very ill indeed and the staff's sleep was being snatched whenever and wherever possible, and meals had been reduced to sandwiches and interminable cups of coffee? George wanted his pound of flesh out of Sean and he was prepared to use any situation to get it.

'Do you have any comment for our readers on the way Dr Maguire is handling the situation?' a voice asked.

'I have no comment to make about anything,' she replied through gritted teeth, well aware of how easily her words could be distorted. 'All I will say is if you don't all stop pushing and shoving like this someone is going to get hurt!'

As though on cue she heard a sharp cry of pain from the centre of the crowd. Instinctively she pulled her emergency medical bag from her car and elbowed her way towards where the sound had come from.

One of the photographers was lying on the ground, blood pouring from his head, and her heart sank. Please let it be something simple, she prayed as she opened her bag. The last thing Sean needed was her bringing a member of the Press into the hospital, even for a short time. Quickly she cleaned the wound and saw with relief that though the gash was deep it wasn't serious.

'Have you had a tetanus injection?' she asked the photographer as she searched through her bag for some steri-strips.

He nodded, white-faced.

'Pity,' she said tersely. 'I would have enjoyed giving you one of those. OK, you'll live,' she added, getting to her feet, 'though I'd advise you to get that checked by your own doctor as soon as you can. And now,' she continued, with a hard glare at the rest of the crowd, 'if I might be allowed to go to work?'

The members of the Press parted reluctantly in front of her and quickly she ran up the steps of the hospital to find the foyer thronged with anxious parents. They crowded towards her immediately, their faces showing the strain of the last few days, but though she'd known some of these parents for years, had treated their children for a variety of complaints, she knew she couldn't linger. All she could do was give them a few reassuring words and then make for Sean's office to hear the latest report on the situation.

'Go right in,' Molly said as soon as she saw her.

'How is he?' Abby could not help but ask.

Molly shrugged expressively and Abby sighed. Sean was pushing himself harder than any of them. He hadn't left the hospital once since the outbreak had occurred, taking what sleep he could get in his office and sending Molly down to his cottage when he needed a change of clothes.

'I see the members of the Press have arrived now,' he said as soon as she opened the door.

'I damn near had to fight my way over them to get in,' she sighed. 'What's the situation this morning?'

'The hospital switchboard's totally jammed and we couldn't make an emergency phone call if our lives depended on it so keep your cellphone with you at all times,' he said grimly. 'I've worried parents stacked everywhere, three more children are showing symptoms, and the health authority are threatening to close us down and transfer all our patients to Inverness. That's what the situation is this morning.'

'It can only get better, then?' she said, trying to smile and failing miserably.

He didn't answer; in fact he seemed a million miles

away and her heart went out to him. His face was
drawn and haggard, his suit was crumpled, his shirt
creased and limp. There was even a nick on the side
of his chin where he must have cut himself shaving
and unaccountably she found herself remembering the
first day they'd met when she'd likened him so dispar-
agingly to a fashion-plate.

There was nothing of the fashion-plate about him
now, nothing at all, and as he looked round at her,
suddenly conscious of her gaze, his vulnerability moved
her more than any words he could have spoken. Gently
she put her hand on his arm.

'We'll get through this somehow—it will be all right;
I just know it will.'

He tilted her chin with his hand and she didn't pull
away. 'You've picked a hell of a situation to suddenly
become kind, Abby.'

The appeal in his grey eyes was clear, the tenderness
on his face unmistakable, and it took a supreme effort
of will not to stretch up and lock her arms around his
neck and kiss him. 'You could do with a change of
shirt if you're going to be meeting the parents,' she
said shakily.

A wry smile crossed his face. 'Always the practical
one, aren't you?' he said, and unbuttoned his shirt and
took it off.

'Would you like me to come back later?' she said
quickly, all too conscious that the sight of his bare
chest was doing nothing for her self-control.

'There's no need,' he said with a sly sidelong glance
in her direction. 'I don't mind if you don't and I'm
only changing my shirt, you'll be relieved to hear.'

There was amusement in his voice and she bit her
lip. It shouldn't have mattered a damn to her if he
had taken off all his clothes. She was a doctor, for
God's sake. She'd seen thousands—well, hundreds

anyway—of completely naked men in her time. But they weren't Sean, a little voice whispered—and their bare chests hadn't reawakened memories that were playing havoc with her blood pressure.

'What's the medical situation at the moment?' she asked, wandering in studied casualness over to his desk, only to stop short with a groan as she caught sight of her reflection in the mirror behind it.

She'd washed her hair before coming back to the hospital this morning and totally forgotten to comb it through and now it was sticking out all over the place in a riot of curls. Vainly she attempted to flatten it down, but suddenly Sean's hands caught hers.

'Leave it alone. I like it like that.'

'It's a nightmare,' she laughed weakly, all too aware of the feel of his bare broad chest against her back. 'I should concede defeat and get the whole damn lot cut off.'

'Over my dead body,' he said firmly, grasping a handful and burying his face in it. 'I love your hair. I love the colour and the thickness and the smell of it.'

'It's supermarket shampoo—beats the hell out of hospital carbolic any day,' she replied, fighting to keep control of herself, fighting to resist the temptation to turn round and cling to that chest. 'The medical situation—you were going to tell me about the hospital situation.'

'Was I?' he said solemnly, and she could see his eyes gleaming in the mirror.

'You were,' she said, neatly sidestepping him.

He sighed and picked up a clean shirt from the seat near him. 'The staff who went off sick at the beginning of this outbreak are making good progress but we've twelve children in various stages of infection. The most serious at the moment are Becky Reid, Christopher

Paterson, John-Robert Munro, Craig Lattimer, and Susan Fielding.'

'But they're all responding to the medication we're giving them, aren't they?'

'Responding, yes, but they're pretty dehydrated and as none of them were very strong to start with it's hitting their systems pretty hard.'

A chill raced through her heart. 'They are all going to get well, aren't they, Sean?' she said uncertainly. 'I mean, it is only a matter of time before they all make a full recovery, isn't it?'

He buttoned his shirt deliberately and didn't meet her eyes. 'You know the score as well as I do, Abby—children can die from Campylobacter.'

She refused to think about that, refused even to contemplate it, and deliberately changed the subject. 'One of the reporters—he said there's to be an emergency board meeting tomorrow—is that true?'

His lips set into a tight line. 'They're looking for a scapegoat, and I guess it's me.'

Her own hurt at the way he had treated her struggled with her sense of injustice and her sense of injustice won.

'But they must know it wouldn't have mattered if a trained chimpanzee had been in charge of the hospital,' she protested. 'This outbreak's got nothing to do with you—you didn't start it.'

'Try telling that to George Benson,' he said ruefully.

'I will—at the meeting tomorrow.'

'It's closed session, Abby—just me and the eleven good men and true. But thanks for offering to champion my cause—even if it does come as a bit of a surprise,' he added meaningfully.

She couldn't meet his steady gaze but her bruised heart cried out in despair. Why couldn't I have been enough for you, Sean? Why do you have to be the kind of man you are? And why—in God's name, why—do I always have to fall in love with men who are going to hurt me?

'Would you like me to see some of the parents for you this morning?' she said quickly. 'Alastair and the nursing staff are coping well with the children and if I'm needed they can send for me.'

'Would you do that for me?' he said, clear relief appearing on his face. 'If we split the parents down the middle we should be able to see all of them by mid-afternoon if we're lucky.'

'I'll tell Molly what we're doing,' she said, walking towards the door.

'Abby?'

She stopped and turned.

'Thanks,' he said simply.

'Hey, us professional colleagues have to stick together in a crisis,' she smiled, and knew with certainty from the look on his face that her reply had disappointed him.

What did he want from her? she wondered wretchedly as she made her way towards her own office. Did he expect her to be available whenever he wanted her? Did he expect her to be content to share him? She shook her head deliberately. No matter how she felt about him, she knew she couldn't do that. For her it had to be all or nothing and she realised, with depressing clarity, that it was going to be nothing.

Seeing the parents was more physically and mentally exhausting than she would ever have imagined possible and she could only guess at how Sean must be feeling after having endured this for three days. The terror in the parents' eyes, their air of grim resignation tore at her, and though she tried to sound positive she knew that nothing she said was easing the fear they felt.

'How many more, Molly?' she sighed wearily after some two and a half hours.

'Just one more in your queue.'

'Who is it?'

'Ben Reid.'

Abby could not hide her surprise. Since that day in Sean's office there had been no word at all from Becky's father and she had begun to believe that Sean's shock tactics hadn't worked any more than her own gentle approach had done.

'I could send him along to Dr Maguire if you'd prefer?' Molly continued, seeing her hesitate.

The last meeting with Ben had been an ugly one and she couldn't deny she was tempted. What had he come here to say? Don't treat Becky; let her die? She couldn't handle that. She knew her temper would snap.

'How many parents has Dr Maguire still to see?' she said slowly.

'Four.'

That settled it. She'd have to see Ben herself, and somehow she'd have to keep her temper.

'Send him in, Molly.'

Quickly she took a steadying breath and that was all she had time to do. Ben Reid came in like a whirlwind.

'I want to know how this could have happened,' he demanded. 'I want to know how patients can come in here to be helped and end up sicker than when they were admitted!'

'The health authority are checking our kitchens and food suppliers are trying to find the source—'

'The newspapers—they said children can die from this infection. Is that true?' he said, cutting across her.

'That can happen, yes,' she said smoothly, conscious of the hectic flush of colour on Ben's face, the wildness in his eyes, 'but Becky is a tough little girl—' She came to a halt, seeing his shoulders sag. 'The medication we're giving her is having some effect and she's doing quite well—'

'Don't give me any of that meaningless crap!' he retorted. 'I want to know the truth—I want—' His face crumpled. 'I don't want her to die, Dr Hunter. God knows I've been a lousy enough father to her all these months but I never wanted her to die!'

Abby took his trembling hands in hers. 'I won't lie to you, Ben. This infection is an extremely serious one but Becky is responding to treatment.'

'Can. . .can I see her?' he whispered.

'You'll have to scrub up and wear protective clothing—we're trying to minimise both the possible risk to you and the risk of the children becoming further infected with something else.'

He nodded slowly. 'I don't care what I have to do as long as I can see her.' She accompanied him to the door and he paused. 'Will you tell Dr Maguire something for me? Will you tell him that—if Becky pulls through this—I want to take her home?'

A wide smile lit up her face. 'Oh, Ben, I'm so glad, so very glad you've come to that decision. It's not going to be easy—you know that, don't you?—but we'll help you all we can and you have such a lovely daughter.'

'Will I still have her after all this is over?' he said, gazing at her searchingly.

'I hope so, Ben,' she said, her throat constricted. 'I hope so.'

After she had taken him along to see Becky Abby made her way slowly down to the nurses' staffroom. Three hours of speaking to parents, three hours of constantly trying to sound positive and encouraging, had drained her totally and what she wanted most was company and diversion, but as soon as she opened the staffroom door she regretted her decision. There was only one nurse in the room—Carol Lennox.

'Hi there,' Carol smiled before she could turn and leave. 'Want a coffee?'

Abby took a deep breath and smiled in return. 'I'd prefer a new body if there's one on offer, Carol.'

'Sorry, but we're fresh out of new bodies at the moment; you'll just have to settle for the coffee,' she chuckled.

Abby took the steaming mug from her gratefully and sat down. 'How's things in Ward 6?' she said with an effort.

'No better, but no worse, thank God. When do you think this is going to end, Abby? Is there any word of where the outbreak originated?'

'Not as far as I know,' Abby replied, kicking off her shoes and stretching out her toes in an attempt to ease the stiffness in her back.

'Dr Maguire's been really wonderful through all this, hasn't he?' Carol observed.

The compliment sent a stab of pain through Abby's heart but she nodded.

'It's amazing how wrong you can be about someone,' Carol continued thoughtfully. 'I mean, when I first saw him I thought, Wow, what a hunk—and then later I found him a bit intimidating. It's only lately—over the last few weeks in fact—that I've realised just how very kind and gentle he can be.'

Abby moistened her lips. She knew she shouldn't ask, she knew she was only going to put herself through further hell by asking, but she couldn't restrain herself. 'So what brought about your conversion?' she said, trying to keep the hurt out of her voice and only just succeeding. 'When did you decide he wasn't so bad after all?'

'When I told him about my mother.'

'Your mother?' Abby said in confusion.

'Robert told you how ill she was, didn't he?' Carol said tremulously. 'They couldn't operate—the cancer was too far advanced—and Dr Maguire found me crying one day and said if I ever needed to talk to someone to come to him. He was so good, Abby. He listened to me, let me cry on his shoulder, and he really seemed to understand. It was almost as though he knew what it was like to lose someone he loved.'

Abby nodded but said nothing. What Sean had told her about his nephew had been in confidence and she couldn't repeat it.

'Actually it could all have got a bit embarrassing,' Carol continued with a deep flush. 'When I heard that my mother had died I was devastated. Robert was away at a meeting and I went to see Dr Maguire and I. . .I ended up kissing him.

'I didn't set out to—and it didn't mean anything, I swear,' she added quickly as Abby sat bolt upright in her seat, all fatigue suddenly gone from her body. 'I just needed some comfort, that's all, and Dr Maguire was great. He didn't read anything into it as a lot of other men might have done. He just said that I'd kissed him as a friend, and he was flattered to be counted as one. Wasn't that nice of him?'

'Yes. . .yes, it was,' Abby said, her voice low.

'You won't tell Robert about this, will you?' Carol said hurriedly. 'I don't think he'd understand—Come to think of it,' she added with a wry chuckle, 'I doubt if I'd understand either if I came across him kissing someone else!'

The door to the staffroom opened and Kate Johnson's head appeared round it. 'Sorry, Carol, but you're wanted back in your ward.'

'No rest for the wicked,' Carol grumbled as she got to her feet. 'Hey, are you OK, Abby?' she added, staring down at her with concern.

'I'm fine—just fine,' Abby replied with difficulty.

So she'd been wrong; she'd been wrong all the time. Sean hadn't been kissing Carol, she'd been kissing him—for comfort's sake. Her heart soared at the thought and then just as quickly tumbled down. How could she explain? How could she possibly justify the dreadful things she'd said to him?

Humble pie time, Abby, she thought with a sigh, and lots of it. She could just imagine what he'd say— he'd never let her hear the end of it. A small smile appeared on her lips as she made for the door. It would be worth it; it would be worth every minute of it.

'Thank goodness—you're the very person I've been looking for,' Molly said with some relief as she came into her office. 'Dr Maguire wants to see you.'

'And I want to see him,' Abby smiled.

'He's in a dreadful mood,' the secretary warned, looking distinctly harassed.

'I think I can cheer him up,' Abby replied.

'Abby—'

But she was talking to thin air. Abby had already gone into Sean's office and Molly crossed her fingers and waited for the explosion she knew was about to come.

'I've been looking for you,' Sean said as soon as he saw her.

'So I hear,' she said, taking a seat. 'I was in the nurses' quarters having a cup of coffee.'

'Not using your cellphone to call the Press?' His voice was cold, biting.

'Why on earth would I be calling the Press?' she said, bewildered.

He threw a newspaper down on the desk between them.

'It's the latest edition,' he said curtly.

'So?' she said, growing even more confused.

'Page two—I think you'll find it interesting.'

She sighed. 'It's not another in-depth report on our Campylobacter outbreak, is it?'

'It is, but this particular report has a new slant to it,' he replied. 'Read it.'

She lifted the newspaper and turned to page two.

'"Pert red-headed Dr Abigail Hunter"—*pert*?' she exclaimed. 'Ye gods, who wrote this rubbish?'

'Not that bit.' His face was grim. 'The second column, halfway down.'

She gazed at him curiously and then obediently started to read further down the page, only to come to a sudden halt. 'But I don't understand—'

'Read it; read all of it,' he ordered.

She did, and with every line she read the colour on her cheeks deepened. It wasn't possible, her brain protested, but there it was. There in black and white was the letter George Benson had wanted her to sign, but she knew that not even he would have been rash enough to release it to the Press without her signature, so how in the world had they got hold of it? And then, with a sinking heart, she remembered.

George had put the letter in her emergency medical bag. She'd always intended to take it out, to tear it to shreds, but so much had happened over the last few weeks that she'd completely forgotten about it. It had been in her bag when she'd treated that photographer this morning. Someone must have pulled it out, thought it too good to ignore, and printed it as though she'd written it.

She cleared her throat. 'I didn't give the Press this—they stole it—'

'You don't deny you wrote it, then?' he interrupted.

'Of course I do,' she retorted, only to see his lips curl in clear disbelief. 'I'll phone them, insist they print a retraction.'

'I'd say the damage was already done, wouldn'
you?' he replied coldly. '"Senior doctor has no confi
dence in her chief of staff"—isn't that what it says?'

'But I didn't write—'

'Sleeping with me—was that just so you could ad(
sexual harassment to your string of complaints?' h(
said bitingly.

The colour drained from her face. 'You can'
believe—'

'I was a fool, wasn't I?' he said, his lips twisting
'You told me when we met you thought you shoul(
have been appointed chief of staff. You made no secre
of the fact that you were ambitious. I should have
realised just how ambitious you were and what length:
you'd go to to get what you wanted. Well, when thi:
is over you can have my job with my blessing—Go(
knows I'd say you've worked hard enough for it!'

She flinched at the contempt in his voice. 'Is tha
what you think of me—is that what you truly think—
that I'd sleep with you to get your job?'

'Why else would you give me the cold-shoulder treat
ment afterwards?' he demanded, his mouth hardening
'You had me running around half-crazy, wondering
what the hell I'd done, and the god-awful truth was I
hadn't done a damn thing. You'd planned all this from
the very beginning, hadn't you?'

'Sean—'

'I have to say I think you sold yourself pretty cheap,
my dear—the chief of staff's job for your long-
protected virginity. Or weren't you a virgin at all just
a damned good actress?'

'How can you say that?' Her voice was little more
than a whisper, her eyes enormous in her white face.
'How can you say that after we. . .after we—? Don'
you trust me at all?'

His face set. 'If you can give me one good reason

why I should I'd be very interested to hear it.'

'There doesn't seem much point in me saying any-thing, does there?' she said, her voice breaking. 'No matter what I say you're not going to believe me, are you? You'd rather believe something you read in a newspaper. Well, thanks, Sean—thanks for nothing!'

She got to her feet stiffly, feeling as though her heart was breaking, and then stood rooted to the spot as the piercing sound of an alarm bell suddenly shattered the still of the office. For a split second neither of them moved and then their eyes swivelled simultaneously to the emergency board.

'Ward 6!' Sean exclaimed.

He tore down the corridor with Abby scarcely a pace behind, both of them knowing that the alarm was only sounded in cases of dire emergency.

When they reached Ward 6 they didn't have to ask why the emergency bell had been sounded. Christopher Paterson had clearly gone into cardiac arrest. Alastair Bell and Carol Lennox were frantically applying CPR to his limp body, both of them knowing that if he wasn't resuscitated within four minutes irre-versible brain damage would occur.

'Have you got him, Carol?' Sean demanded.

'Only just, Dr Maguire,' she replied breathlessly.

'Right, Theatre—now!' Sean ordered. 'And don't stop the CPR.'

Quickly they wheeled Christopher out of the ward, past the terrified faces of the other children, and then ran like the wind towards the operating theatre. Time was of the essence and they all knew it, just as everyone knew the part they had to play in such an emergency.

'Heartbeat, Alastair?' Sean questioned once they were in the theatre, glancing over his shoulder at him as he inserted an intravenous line.

'Erratic,' he replied, his gaze fixed on the monitor

that was linked to the electrodes he'd attached to Christopher's body, and then he swore under his breath. 'He's arresting again, Sean!'

'Any pulse, Abby?' Sean said, turning to her.

'None,' she answered unevenly, 'and his pupils are dilating.'

'OK,' he said, 'paddles, please.'

She handed them to him with trembling fingers.

'Everyone clear?' he asked, raising his head.

Obediently they all stood back from the trolley as Sean applied one paddle to either side of Christopher's heart and Abby prayed as she had never prayed before as the small body jerked and convulsed from the electrical surge.

'Anything?' Sean demanded.

Alastair shook his head. 'No change.'

Again Sean applied the paddles, again Christopher's body jerked and convulsed, and again Alastair shook his head when Sean turned in his direction.

For what seemed like hours but was in reality only minutes Sean repeated the procedure, until at last he straightened up wearily and shook his head.

'OK, thanks, everyone, but that's it.'

Abby gazed at him in protest. 'Why are you stopping? You can't just stop.'

'He's dead, Abby,' he said flatly.

'No. *No*.' Her voice was a high-pitched wail as she grabbed the paddles from his hands and pushed him aside. 'Stand clear, everyone.'

'Abby, this is useless—'

'Stand clear, damn you!' she cried. 'I won't let you give up on him—you've got to keep on trying.'

'Abby, he's dead,' he said gently, motioning to Alastair to switch off the current. 'He's *dead*.'

'One more try—just one more try,' she said insistently, shrugging off his restraining hand.

'Abby, he hasn't been breathing now for six minutes. You've got to accept it—we've lost him.'

She shook her head determinedly. 'No—not Christopher, not Christopher.'

Gently he prised the paddles from her clenched fingers. 'I'm sorry, Abby, I'm so very sorry.'

She gazed down at Christopher's small, limp body and a half-sob broke from her. 'His parents—what am I going to tell his parents?'

'I'll tell them.'

'Will you?' she murmured, staring at him unseeingly. 'That's kind—that's kind.'

'Abby—'

'We never did take him back to Cawdor,' she said, her voice cracking. 'He never did get to see his ducks again. Oh, Sean, he said people thought he was a freak because he had cerebral palsy, but he wasn't a freak, he was just a little boy—just a little boy!'

Scalding hot tears rolled down her cheeks and he stared at her helplessly, knowing that though part of him wanted to reach out and take her in his arms and comfort her the other part could not forget that damning letter in the newspaper.

She gazed up at him, knowing that she'd never needed him as much as she needed him right now, but there was indecision in his face and she took a step towards him.

'Sean, *please*!'

Her cry was a desperate, heart-rending appeal, but almost imperceptibly she saw him shake his head and with a racking sob she ran blindly from the theatre.

CHAPTER TEN

A HEAVY silence hung over the wards and corridors of Ardmar the next day. The death of any patient was a sad event but Christopher had been a particularly popular child and many tried to extend their sympathy to Abby only to meet with a curt nod and a white face.

'I guess his heart just couldn't stand the strain, Abby,' Kate Johnson said sympathetically when Abby called in on Ward 1 to see how Craig Lattimer was progressing. 'A ruptured appendix is dangerous enough for a child like Christopher and for him then to contract Campylobacter on top of it. . . His death wasn't anyone's fault—'

'Oh, it was someone's fault, Kate,' Abby said bitterly. 'That infected food came from somewhere and I hope whoever produced it rots in hell!'

Kate shuffled her charts awkwardly for a moment. 'Everyone's saying the board of governors are going to ask Dr Maguire for his resignation this morning,' she said at last. 'That he's going to be made to carry the can for the outbreak.'

'That's absolute rubbish,' Abby said tersely. 'The board can't force him to resign. There's not a court in the land that could convict him of negligence—he didn't produce the food or cook it, for God's sake!'

Kate opened her mouth and then closed it again.

'How's Craig this morning?' Abby continued more evenly.

'Slightly better. The drip is keeping his fluid intake up and he's not showing any sign of dehydration.'

172

'Thank God for that,' Abby replied. 'And his temperature?'

'It's gone down a degree. Dr Maguire thinks the infection could be peaking at last.'

Abby said nothing. She had seen Sean only briefly before he'd gone off to his meeting with the board and they hadn't spoken. They'd been like two strangers, she thought wretchedly, and then unconsciously she shook her head. It had been worse than that. Strangers would at least have been able to make some kind of conversation, talk about generalities if nothing else. They hadn't even been able to do that.

Aware that Kate was staring at her, she squared her shoulders. The crisis wasn't over yet; there were other children who were still quite seriously ill, and she had a job to do.

'Let's hope Dr Maguire is right,' she said, moving on to the next patient. 'That this is all going to be over very soon.'

'I think it's going to be all over sooner rather than later for Dr Maguire,' Kate muttered, thinking of the meeting that was taking place above them.

Ardmar's board of governors were all solid middle-class pillars of the local community, and to a man they were worried. None of them had escaped the attentions of the local and national press and they were looking for a scapegoat—any scapegoat.

Sean could see it in their eyes as they trooped silently into the boardroom and a grim smile passed over his lips. If they wanted his resignation he wasn't going to argue. He wasn't going to point out that what they were asking was not only unfair but also unethical. He would give them his resignation because he quite simply no longer cared.

'I think we all know why we're here today, gentlemen,' George Benson declared, his small brown eyes showing his enjoyment of the situation as he gazed around the room. 'Grave situations call for grave measures but in fairness to Dr Maguire I think each and everyone of us should put forward our point of view.'

Uncomfortably, awkwardly, each member of the board spoke in turn and as the words 'inefficient', 'negligent', 'incompetent' echoed round the room Sean's mind drifted.

He had spent a sleepless night, tormented by the look on Abby's face when she had begged him for comfort after Christopher's death and he hadn't given it. If only he could turn the clock back; if only he could have forgotten that wretched letter just for one minute.

But it was too late, too late. She would never forgive him, and why should she when he had mistrusted her on the strength of something in a newspaper? Everyone knew that newspapers constantly twisted stories for publicity and he hadn't even given her the opportunity to explain. He'd behaved no better than the men who were judging him now.

He clenched his pen tightly between his fingers as other memories surfaced—of that night in her cottage, of her body, shy and uncertain in his arms. She had been a virgin when she'd given herself to him; of that he was certain. No one was that good an actress; no one could have faked so convincingly the look of wonder on her face when he'd entered her.

But why had she treated him as she had afterwards? God, she'd even said she hated him. Why had she done that—*why*, if she hadn't wanted his job?

'Perhaps you'd like to say a few words now in your own defence, Dr Maguire?' George Benson asked, interrupting his thoughts.

'In my defence?' Sean echoed. 'I wasn't aware

this was a court of law, Mr Benson.'

An ugly flush of colour appeared on George's face. 'Do you want to say a few words or not, Dr Maguire?'

Sean sighed. He knew that short of some amazing act of God he was out of a job, but he supposed he'd better go through the motions of appearing interested and slowly he got to his feet.

'Good grief, they're not still talking, are they, Molly?' Abby said in some surprise as she came into the outer office some time later with her morning reports to find the secretary with her ear firmly planted to the boardroom door.

'It's been almost an hour now,' Molly replied, 'and before you ask—no, I can't hear a damn word!'

Abby chuckled. 'What on earth are they finding to talk about?'

'I don't know,' the secretary answered. 'I wouldn't have thought it would take them this long to ask him to resign.'

Abby stared at her. 'But they can't do that—they haven't got a leg to stand on.'

'Of course they haven't!' Molly exclaimed. 'But he said if they asked for his resignation he was going to give it to them. He just doesn't seem to care any more, Abby, even though if he resigns from here it will probably mean the end of his career. You know what people are like—the mud will stick. Everyone will say there's no smoke without fire.'

Abby sat down limply. No matter what her private feelings about him were, Sean had been good for Ardmar. He was an excellent doctor and a first-rate administrator. Good God, he had even managed to ensure sufficient funding for the hospital's survival, which was more than William Lawrie had ever managed.

Why was he throwing in the towel like this? Why wasn't he putting up a fight? It wasn't his fault there had been an outbreak of Campylobacter. It could have happened anywhere and surely he must know that.

'Abby.' Molly looked decidedly uncomfortable. 'I have a problem.'

'Something I can help with?' she said with an effort, pushing her thoughts to the back of her mind.

'This came by special courier from the health authority about half an hour ago,' Molly replied, holding up a sealed envelope.

Abby stared at it. 'Do you think it's got anything to do with the source of the outbreak, Molly?'

'That's what I'm wondering. I'd open it but it's marked "private and confidential"—for the attention of Dr Maguire only.'

'You could take it in to him,' Abby suggested, but Molly shook her head.

'I can't. The board said they were not to be interrupted under any circumstances unless it was a case of dire emergency—like the hospital going on fire. If I go in with that and it turns out to be nothing important I'll really get hauled over the coals.'

The two women gazed uncertainly at the envelope and Abby made up her mind. 'Give it here,' she said, and tore it open.

'Well?' Molly said nervously as Abby scanned the letter. 'Put me out of my misery, for God's sake—is it important?'

A wave of bitter anger surged through Abby. 'Oh, it's important all right,' she said, walking deliberately towards the boardroom door. 'Very important.'

The board of governors swung round in surprise at her entrance but the first person to speak was, predictably, George Benson.

'This is a closed meeting, Dr Hunter,' he declared,

bristling visibly. 'You have no right to be here, no right at all!'

'I'm sorry for this intrusion, gentlemen,' she said, smiling round at them all, 'but some new information has come to light.'

'I think we have all the facts we require,' George blustered. 'We were just about to take a vote of confidence on Dr Maguire's handling of the current situation—'

'But surely you wouldn't want to do that without being in full possession of the facts?' Abby interrupted smoothly. 'The health authority have identified the source of the infection and I think you should know where it came from before you take any vote.'

The board members looked at one another uncertainly and George glared at her. 'This is most unorthodox, Dr Hunter, most unorthodox! The source of the outbreak has no bearing at all on what we have come here to discuss—'

'I think you'll find it has quite considerable bearing, Mr Benson,' she said. 'Correct me if I'm wrong,' she added, staring pointedly round the table, 'but I was under the impression that this was a board meeting, not a one-man judge and jury?'

One or two of the board members nodded and someone murmured, 'I think we should hear what the health authority say.'

A ripple of agreement ran round the room and quickly she handed Sean the letter. 'I think you're going to enjoy this, Dr Maguire,' she said, and as his eyebrows rose questioningly she swung on her heel and went out of the room.

'What happened?' Molly declared.

Abby put her finger to her lips and waited. Not a sound could be heard, not a murmur, and then suddenly there was total uproar.

'What on earth was in that letter?' Molly asked, her green eyes sparkling with keen curiosity.

'You'll find out soon enough,' Abby smiled, refusing to be drawn.

But her smile did not last long. Bitterness took its place as she walked towards her office—bitterness and regret and anger. The Campylobacter infection had come from chickens—chickens supplied by George Benson's firm. Christopher had died because George had been cutting corners, not following government health guidelines, in an attempt to maximise his profits.

If Christopher hadn't died she would have relished seeing George Benson being humbled, enjoyed watching him being forced to resign—and he would have to resign. His credibility and social standing would be shattered once the Press got hold of that report. Now she felt nothing at all but a dull ache in her heart at the needlessness of it all and a desperate loneliness as she forced herself to stare into the future.

With luck, the outbreak at Ardmar had peaked and there would be no more deaths. Life at the hospital would gradually return to normal, but she couldn't continue working here. Even if she could persuade Sean that she hadn't written the letter they couldn't go back to the way they were. He hadn't believed her and she hadn't trusted him and how could there be love if there was no trust?

She could picture herself all too clearly, never being one hundred per cent sure of him, watching him smiling at a pretty girl and wondering, listening to him laugh with someone attractive and growing suspicious. Michael hadn't just humiliated her, she realised; he had left her incapable of trusting anyone.

With a sigh she went into her office, threaded a sheet of paper into her typewriter and began to type her resignation.

She had just finished when the door was thrown open and Sean walked in, clear elation on his face.

'When you stage a dramatic scene, Abby Hunter, you sure as heck know how to stage one!' he exclaimed. 'When I read out that letter all hell broke loose.'

'I heard,' she smiled, signing her letter and putting it into an envelope.

'You should have stayed, shared the moment when George resigned with me,' he declared.

'Quite frankly I think the whole board should have resigned,' she replied. 'None of them showed any independent thought. They all just followed George's lead like the load of gutless, spineless sheep they are.'

'The board have suggested we ask Finlay Norris to take George's place.'

'I'd say that's the only sensible thing they've done this morning,' she said.

He paced the floor, his face alight and excited. 'It's going to be all right now—Ardmar—it's really going to start going places. With Finlay on our side, the trust fund up and running, we can think about expansion, maybe adding another wing.'

'I wish you all the luck in the world,' she said, holding out her envelope to him.

'What's this?' he asked, taking it from her outstretched hand and staring curiously down at it. 'Not more revelations about George, is it?' he added with a grin.

'It's my resignation.'

The smile was wiped from his face instantly. 'You're joking, I hope?'

'Perfectly serious,' she replied evenly. 'From what I can remember my contract insists I work out three months' notice but I'd be grateful if you could let me go as soon as you find someone to replace me.'

He threw the letter down on her desk. 'I won't accept it.'

'You haven't got any choice, Sean.'

Deliberately he picked up the envelope and tore it in two.

'That was pretty pointless,' she sighed. 'I'm just going to have to type it all over again.'

'But *why*, Abby, why should you want to leave?' His voice was incredulous.

Her heart thudded against her chest. Why couldn't he just have made this easy for her? Why couldn't he just have accepted it without question? 'I need a change of scene, Sean, new faces, new challenges, and I think now's as good a time as any for me to start afresh.'

'But the hospital needs you,' he protested.

She shook her head. 'I'm a good pair of hands but I'm not indispensable—no one is.'

'You've invested six years of your life here—don't throw it all away just because I accused you of. . .of. . .'

'Sleeping with you to get your job?' she finished for him, and saw him wince. 'I don't want your job, Sean—I don't even think, if I'm honest, I could do it.

'And for the record George Benson wrote that letter,' she added as he made to speak. 'He brought it into my office one morning, wanting me to sign it. I refused but he put it into my emergency medical bag, saying I should take time to consider the situation. I meant to take it out, to burn it, but I forgot. Do you remember when one of the photographers got hurt in the scrum outside the hospital?'

'I remember.'

'When I was treating him my bag was wide open to the skies. Some reporter must have seen the letter, swiped it, thought it would make wonderful headline news, and you know the rest of the story.'

He raked a hand through his hair. 'Why didn't you tell me?'

'You didn't want to hear anything I had to say if you recall,' she said wryly. 'Don't look so stricken, Sean,' she added. 'It doesn't matter any more.'

'But it does matter!' he flared. 'When I think of how I treated you after Christopher died. . .' Her face twisted slightly and he caught her hand. 'Then why—if it wasn't my job you wanted—did you behave as you did after we made love, shutting me out, telling me what we did meant nothing?'

With a supreme effort of will she pulled her hand from his. 'It was another case of jumping to conclusions—this time on my part.'

'Tell me.'

She coloured. 'I thought—I saw you with Carol—the morning after we'd made love. She was kissing you and I thought—'

'Oh, Abby, you idiot!' he said, reaching for her, only to see her step back.

'It doesn't matter any more—don't you see that?' she said, her face bleak. 'We should have been able to trust one another—if we truly loved one another we would have trusted one another but we didn't.'

'So we've made mistakes—we're only human,' he said, his voice raw with emotion. 'Can't we just forget what happened, start again?'

'And what about the next time?' she said dully.

'There will be no next time,' he insisted, gripping her by the shoulders.

His closeness was unbearable, her need for him as strong as ever, and she swallowed hard. 'Maybe not for you, but I don't think I'm capable of trusting anyone—not fully.'

'Why are you doing this to yourself—to me?' he demanded, his face taut.

'Because I know myself better than you do and that's why I'm leaving, Sean,' she said sadly.

His hands dropped from her shoulders. 'There's nothing I can say to make you change your mind?'

'No.' Her voice was a whisper.

In the days that followed something like normality slowly began to return to Ardmar as one by one the children's health gradually improved and they were pronounced out of danger. With no story to follow the Press left the grounds and laid siege to George Benson's factory instead, hoping for a glimpse of the owner, who had suddenly become decidedly reclusive, but George would have needed to search long and hard to find anyone who had any sympathy for him.

'I hope they lock him in jail and throw away the key,' Ben Reid declared as he wheeled his daughter out to his car one morning.

'I doubt it, but I have every sympathy with your feelings, Ben,' Abby replied. 'You'll keep in touch with us, won't you?' she added, stroking Becky's blonde hair lightly as her father lifted her into the car and then stowed her wheelchair in the boot.

'Try keeping us away,' he smiled.

He looked ten years younger. There was a spring in his step and a lightness about his shoulders. No one could pretend that the future was going to be easy for either him or Becky but they had taken the first step and with the back-up services Ardmar could give them the road would be that little bit smoother.

'You must be pleased with your success story?' a voice said as she watched Ben's car drive away.

'I can't take the credit for this one, Jean,' she smiled,

turning to face her. 'Sean's macho approach won on this occasion.'

'I understand Craig Lattimer's to be discharged tomorrow—isn't he the last of the children who contracted Campylobacter to go home?'

Abby nodded. 'Yes, but we're keeping John-Robert in for a while. Sean thinks he's located a possible donor for a bone-marrow transplant and if the match is good John-Robert's parents have given us the OK for another try.'

'I hope it works this time,' Jean said fervently.

'So do I.'

'Then why not stay on and find out?' Jean suggested.

A small smile appeared on Abby's face. 'I don't think so, Jean.'

'You're making the wrong decision, you know,' she observed.

'I'm thirty years old, Jean. I left school, went to university, did my hospital practice, and then I came here—all pretty predictable stuff. I'd say it was about time I did something reckless, out of character, don't you?'

Jean's expression was severe. 'There's being reckless and there's being downright stupid, my dear. You've been wandering round this hospital looking like a pale ghost for the last two weeks, and Sean's been going round biting everyone's head off. Isn't it about time the two of you sorted yourselves out?'

'We have—that's why I'm leaving.'

'To do what—to go where?'

'I've got plans—don't worry about me,' was all Abby would say and Jean gave up and went to her car, shaking her head with exasperation.

In truth Abby had made no plans at all. Vaguely she supposed she would take a long holiday in the sun and then start applying for jobs at other children's hospitals but that was as far as her thoughts had taken her. All she knew was that she wanted to get as far away from Ardmar as she could, as far away from Sean as possible. She knew she would never love anyone as much as she loved him but she knew too that she couldn't live a life of uncertainty, a life of doubt and suspicion.

'Abby, my dear, how very nice to see you!' Finlay Norris exclaimed as she came down the corridor towards him.

'It's nice to see you too, Finlay,' she replied, genuinely pleased to see him. 'Are you looking for Sean?'

He grimaced slightly. 'I've just escaped from him. He's been working on me all morning, trying to persuade me to join the board of governors, and frankly I can think of at least a hundred things I'd far rather do than sit on my backside once a month listening to a load of old windbags mouthing off about something they know damn all about.'

'But you're going to do it?' she pressed.

He nodded. 'Sean's pretty persuasive when he wants to be.' He paused. 'Which makes it all the sadder he's leaving.'

'Leaving?' she exclaimed.

'His resignation couldn't have come at a worse time,' he continued. 'Replacing you is going to be hard enough but replacing him as well is going to be pretty damn impossible.'

'But he never said he was leaving—he didn't tell me he'd resigned,' she said quickly.

'I didn't think he had,' Finlay declared, his kind blue eyes fixed on her.

'Did he say why—did he give you any explanation?' she asked.

'All he said was that he was resigning for personal reasons and I'm guessing you're the personal reasons.'

She flushed slightly. 'You're wrong there, Finlay.'

He shook his head. 'Judging by his face you haven't got the monopoly on hurting at the moment, my dear. If ever there was a man who was unhappily in love it's Sean Maguire.'

He was watching her closely and she couldn't meet his eyes. 'Some things just aren't meant to be, Finlay,' she said, her voice low.

A deep sigh came from him. 'Look, I wouldn't ask you to do this normally but could you have a word with him, try and convince him to stay?'

She gazed at him in dismay. 'I couldn't. . .what would I say?'

'How about telling him he's the best man for the job, that the hospital needs his expertise?'

She bit her lip. 'It does. Ardmar will flourish under him.'

'Then tell him that, for Ardmar's sake,' Finlay urged. 'And it's not too late for you if you want to withdraw your resignation.'

She smiled up at him. 'I'll do my best to persuade him to stay on, Finlay, but I've made up my mind and I won't change it.'

'Fair enough, my dear,' he said resignedly, 'but you make a good team and you're going to be hard to replace.'

She walked slowly up the stairs after Finlay had gone, wishing she'd never agreed to his request to talk to Sean. As though by some unspoken agreement they had been avoiding one another for the last two weeks and when they'd met their conversations had been strictly limited to hospital matters.

What could she possibly say to Sean that Finlay hadn't tried already? she thought as she walked reluctantly along the corridor towards his office. He would be quite justified in telling her it was none of her business and that she should just butt out of his life.

Tell the truth, Abby, she thought as she stared uncertainly at the office door. You don't want to do this because you don't want to be alone with him, not even for a minute.

'Coming to see me?'

She jumped back, fighting with her mounting colour, as Sean suddenly opened the door and almost collided with her. 'I wanted a word but it can wait—'

'Come in.'

Slowly she followed him through to his office, all too conscious as she always was of the effect that just his nearness had on her.

'Take a seat and tell me what I can do for you,' he said, perching on the edge of his desk.

She didn't sit down. She stood with her back to the door, knowing she needed its support. 'Finlay told me you're resigning.'

'That's right.'

'But why?' she demanded. 'I thought you were happy here, settled—what's changed?'

'You're not going to be here,' he said simply. 'Oh, Abby, how can I stay in a place where everywhere I go has memories of you, reminders of you?'

She gripped her hands together tightly. He might mean that now but he wouldn't always mean it; she knew that.

'Then forget me, Sean,' she said. 'You're the best damn administrator Ardmar's ever had; you can't just walk away.'

'Like you said, no one's indispensable—the hospital will get by.'

'Oh, for heaven's sake don't be so bloody humble!' she exclaimed angrily. 'It doesn't suit you.'

A glimmer of a smile appeared on his face. 'Your communication skills are slipping, Abby.'

Despite herself a small chuckle was drawn from her. 'So much for me promising Finlay I'd talk you round,' she sighed. 'All I've ended up doing is shouting at you.'

'The first time we met we argued,' he said reflectively.

'Nothing much has changed, has it?' she observed.

'A lot has,' he said. 'I came here with a whole load of emotional and chauvinistic baggage and I've shed it. I've changed and I think you have too.'

Jean had told her she had changed, and if changing meant you hurt as much as she did then she guessed she had.

'Don't leave Ardmar, Abby. Stay—stay with me. I'm asking you—I'm begging you.'

She shook her head, her throat tight. 'I can't. You and me—it just wouldn't work. The first time some gorgeous blonde-haired nurse with legs up to her armpits and breasts out to here walked into Ardmar I'd start to wonder.'

'I'd wonder too if anyone looking even remotely like that walked into Ardmar,' he grinned. 'I'd wonder how she was managing to stay upright with breasts that size!'

'Oh, you know what I mean,' she protested.

'I do, and because I do I want to get two things into that very thick skull of yours,' he said firmly, coming towards her and capturing her hands in his. 'Number one—I'm not Michael. I won't cheat on you, lie to you or hurt you. Number two—no one could walk through that door who is more beautiful than you are.'

She shook her head. 'I'm not beautiful, Sean.'

'You are to me,' he said, tracing her face with his fingers. 'To me you're the most beautiful, aggravating, desirable woman in the whole world. I want to marry you, Abby Hunter.'

'Marry me?' she echoed.

'That's what people usually do when they're in love,

don't they?' he said. 'And I do love you, Abby. Trust
me; love me.'

She gazed into his face and saw the love, the tenderness, the caring there and her heart turned over.
'Sean—'

'There are no guarantees in life, no certainties,
acushla,' he murmured. 'All I can say is that I want
to spend the rest of my life loving you. Marry me,
please.'

'I thought you weren't the marrying kind,' she said
uncertainly.

'I wasn't until I met you,' he replied. 'I wasn't until
somehow you argued and fought and crept your way
into my heart and now I can't imagine my life without
you—I don't *want* to imagine my life without you,
acushla.'

'That word—acushla—what does it mean?' she
asked, and as he gave a small smile she gazed at him
suspiciously. 'If it means idiot, Sean Maguire, I'll make
you sorry.'

He shook his head and laughed. 'You might sometimes behave like an idiot but acushla is an Irish word
for darling.'

'Oh.'

'Yes "oh",' he smiled. 'I'm thirty-six years old,
Abby. I've not led a celibate life by any means and
for the last fifteen years I've never shared my home
with anyone for longer than six months.' He paused.
'I guess what I'm trying to say is I could be difficult
to live with.'

'I'd say downright impossible would be closer to the
mark,' she said.

A grin appeared on his lips and then was gone. 'I'll
never hurt you, Abby; I'll never give you cause to
doubt me. I'll keep you safe.'

'Fight off all dragons for me?' she smiled.

'Every single one of them,' he said firmly. 'Oh, acushla, I want to do crazy things for you; I want to give you the sun, the moon and the stars.'

She stared up at him, at the face she knew almost as well as her own. He was right. There were no certainties in life, no guarantees, and she loved him; she loved him so much. Surely, with his help, she could learn to trust too? She made up her mind.

'I don't want the sun, the moon and the stars, Sean,' she said softly. 'I'll settle just for you if you're on offer.'

'Does that mean yes—that you'll marry me?' he said, his eyes fixed on her.

'Yes, it means yes,' she whispered, and he drew her into his arms and kissed her with a depth and passion that left her breathlessly clinging to him.

'What time do you finish today?' he murmured into her hair.

'Not until six,' she sighed into his chest. 'My boss is a real slave-driver.'

A deep chuckle came from him. 'Then how about I come round to your place at about seven? We could share a meal and then maybe do a little more ice-skating if you like.'

Her lips twitched slightly but she managed to remain solemn. 'I'd like that very much.'

'I was thinking. . .' he continued, nibbling her ear thoughtfully. 'Now that you've graduated from the novice class I could teach you one or two rather intricate new moves if you're interested.'

She gazed up at him. 'Difficult, are they?' she said, her eyes dancing.

'Fiendishly difficult, I'm afraid,' he continued, a slow smile creeping across his face. 'In fact I wouldn't be at all surprised if we had to practise all night just to get them right.'

A bubble of laughter broke from her. 'Is that a promise?'

'The way I'm feeling right now, Abby Hunter,' he replied, cupping her face in his hands and kissing her again, 'that's not a promise, it's a cast-iron certainty!'

And as she locked her fingers round his neck and returned his kiss she decided that under Sean's tuition ice-skating was undoubtedly going to turn out to be her very favourite activity.

FREE

Return this coupon and we'll send you 4 Medical Romance™ novels and a mystery gift absolutely FREE! We'll even pay the postage and packing for you.

We're making you this offer to introduce you to the benefits of Reader Service: FREE home delivery of brand-new Medical Romance novels, at least a month before they are available in the shops, FREE gifts and a monthly Newsletter packed with information.

Accepting these FREE books and gift places you under no obligation to buy, you may cancel at any time, even after receiving just your free shipment. Simply complete the coupon below and send it to:

MILLS & BOON® READER SERVICE, FREEPOST, CROYDON, SURREY, CR9 3WZ.

No stamp needed

Yes, please send me 4 free Medical Romance novels and a mystery gift. I understand that unless you hear from me, I will receive 4 superb new titles every month for just £2.10* each postage and packing free. I am under no obligation to purchase any books and I may cancel or suspend my subscription at any time, but the free books and gifts will be mine to keep in any case. (I am over 18 years of age)

2EP6D

Ms/Mrs/Miss/Mr _____

Address _____

_____

_____ Postcode _____